LEBANON LODGE

ff

DESMOND HOGAN

Lebanon Lodge

faber and faber
LONDON · BOSTON

First published in 1988
by Faber and Faber Limited
3 Queen Square London WC1N 3AU
This paperback edition first published in 1989

Photoset by Wilmaset Birkenhead Wirral
Printed in Great Britain by
Richard Clay Ltd Bungay Suffolk
All rights reserved

British Library Cataloguing in Publication Data

Hogan, Desmond
Lebanon Lodge.
I. Title
823'.914 [F]   PR6058.0346

ISBN 0-571-15313-5

To Barbara

And when I say I 'fear' don't let it disturb you, dearest heart. We all fear when we are in waiting-rooms. Yet we must pass beyond them, and if the other can keep calm, it is all the help we can give each other.

Katherine Mansfield

Contents

Acknowledgements

Some of the stories in this volume have previously appeared in the following publications:

'Lebanon Lodge' in *Image*; 'Elysium' in *Fiction* Magazine and *London Tales*, ed. Julian Evans, Hamish Hamilton; 'The Tipperary Fanale' in *The Best of Fiction*, ed. Judy Cooke, J. M. Dent; 'The Airedale' in *The Literary Review* and *Ireland's Living Voices*, Rainbow; 'Players' in *Woman's Journal* and *Winter's Tales 2*, ed. Robin Baird-Smith, Constable; 'Martyrs' in *The Irish Times* and *Best Stories of 1986*, ed. David Hughes and Giles Gordon, Heinemann; 'Recovery' in *The Irish Times* and *Modern Irish Stories*, ed. Caroline Walsh, Irish Times Publications; 'A Marriage in the Country' read by the author on Radio 3; 'Ties' in *New Fiction I*, P.E.N. ed. Peter Ackroyd, *Quartet*, *Christopher Street* (USA) and read by author on Radio 3; 'Grief' in *2 Plus 2*, ed. James Gill, Mylabris Press; and 'The Vicar's Wife' in *Winter's Tales 3*, ed. Robin Baird-Smith, Constable.

Lebanon Lodge

The house became the property of a member of the ruling party in the Irish parliament in the mid-1970s. With its name definitively written on one of the gate posts it was clear that that name, thought of in innocence – 'The trees of the Lord are full of sap: the cedars of Lebanon which he hath planted' – had become a kind of public chalking-up area, in the minds of those who lived in the vicinity of Dun Laoghaire, County Dublin, for the emotional reverberations of events in one of the world's worst trouble-spots; that name placed on the gate post was a parallel to a stretch of the front page of a newspaper which seared even the minds of these complacent suburban citizens. A lethargic middle-aged woman in a summer dress, her shopping beside her, often paused vacuously beside it. What did it make her think of? Miles away and years away in London, Lucien often fancied he was mentally writing its story as he would the story of a house in the Catholic primary school he attended in Dun Laoghaire for a while – this was a favourite task given by Christian Brothers to nubile, teetering boys, 'A house tells its story', the irony of these Christian Brothers telling Lucien what to do being of course that he was Jewish. What did a house remember in inchoate nights in Maida Vale, London? What secrets did its night-time bougainvillaea and arbutus protect? In a sentence the history of an Irish Jewish family and particularly the history of a young man who had escaped from that family and from the country that family had adopted. 'Alas, poor Erin! thou are thyself an eternal badge of sufferance, the blood of my people rests not on thy head.' Lucien often awoke in the night and imagined he was the receptacle for a history that was greater than him and yet which had defined his own personality. Words, sentences, phrases of folklore came back; it was all built on legend of course, this history, but as he grew older Lucien, insurance broker, decided that he needed legend more and more, not just to escape but to sort out the bits of himself that Ireland had mangled and thrown into confusion – right up to an outwardly successful middle age.

The country his family had come to had been a strange one for Jews; they had come and gone since the beginning of the sixteenth century; Jews had been good spies for Cromwell; Jews had been jesters, travellers on the roads of Ireland – no one knew if they were spies for the English or the French around the time of the planned French invasions at the end of the eighteenth century – Jews had shifted in and out of Jewish identity, not just on the roads of Ireland. There was a time when a whole spate of people, who had presented themselves as pious Catholics when it was difficult and even dangerous to be a pious Catholic, declared themselves to be Jewish on their deaths and asked for internment in the Jewish cemetery in Ballybough. Ballybough, a place by the sea, before it was a Jewish cemetery had been a burial place for suicides. Earth from Israel was imported into Dublin in the eighteenth century for Jewish burials, a handful of it thrown in after the corpse. Wine made from raisins was drunk on feast days and searches were made for tombstones, always disappearing and ending up as hearthstones on sale in market places, albeit hearthstones with Hebrew lettering – this story a comedy among Dublin working-class raconteurs. To this country came the Hoagmans, but not until after the synagogue at Mary's Abbey had been opened and a small bit of stability attained for Irish Jews, a symbol of stability in the new synagogue.

Where the Hoagmans began from was a mystery but there was no doubt where parlour legend allocated their beginnings – a fiercely black-haired woman left Hungary in Napoleonic times and met a man called Hoagman in Southern Bohemia, who had to flee his community – adhesive for false teeth which failed to adhere the teeth to the gum, brightly striped marionettes whose legs and arms quickly fell off, little, charred black Christs that quickly fell off their crosses – a marriage ceremony taking place before she fled with him to London. There they had two children, two boys, and it was the Famine of the 1840s which sent them to Ireland, all those Aid for Ireland events where Mrs Hoagman often got jobs serving soup or mopping marquee floors or attending the lavatorial areas, events so lavish and inspiring that they made you want to go to the land of reputed Famine, so loved did it seem by queens – who came in their carriages; by opera singers – who sang in cherry-coloured dresses on small improvised stages; by marchionesses – who baked huge, escalating cakes which were always threatening to fall, snowy, discreet Alpine peaks on those cakes; and by painters – who slapped people's portraits on in a few minutes.

It was not just this of course which made them go to Ireland – the glamour suggested by Ireland by way of people's eagerness to show their concern for it – but the fact that an Irishman was Jewry's greatest champion, Daniel O'Connell, and that Ireland's great leaders had always seemed to put a word in for the Jews as well as the Catholic Irish. It was a pull to a land promised by Famine aid events and by benevolent, languorous speeches from Irish leaders.

The city they arrived in was reeling under the Famine but still time was taken off to elaborately describe ladies' dresses at Castle balls in the newspapers. That was Mrs Hoagman's first impression of Ireland. A description of a young woman's dress, the woman dying a week after the dress description appeared when her coach fell into the canal near Portobello Barracks. In the early 1850s, when the Hoagmans found their feet, marionettes representing people with Jewish features were sold by women at College Green, and Dublin was held in the thrall of the legend of Pencil Cohen, a Jewish millionaire who'd started a halfpenny pencil industry and yet who slept under newspaper pages, visited and marvelled at by the ladies of Jewish relief organizations, an abundantly rich man who insisted on being a Rathmines Job. Magiash Hoagman, who'd started a small, spice-box industry, soon had his own legend among the children of Chancery Street:

Magpie, Magpie sitting on the sty.
Who, o who has the dirty, greedy eye?

Ireland's tolerance for the Jews was even more considerably in
doubt when a Passionist father ranted from his pulpit that the
Dublin Jews had the crimson mark of deicide on their foreheads.
One of Mr Hoagman's sons stayed in Dublin and one disappeared into the country and was never heard of by him again.

At this point Lucien, in London, would pause. So many
unanswered questions, so many bits that didn't hang together.
But that had been the legend. And Pencil Cohen had indeed
lived. Another Dublin Jewish industrialist with the name Cohen
was called Fresser Cohen to distinguish him from his counter-
part but he couldn't live down the connection after Pencil
Cohen's death, people eager for the continuance of the legend,
and he eventually left Dublin. But Mr Hoagman was thriving
then and there was no question of the Hoagmans, those that
remained in Dublin, leaving this city. They'd found an unexpected base under low, mellifluous, rainy mountains.

Every event concerning themselves was a legend among the
Jews of Dublin when Lucien was growing up – the night the
new synagogue on Adelaide Road was opened in 1892, 'a night
of snow', the night of the Day of Atonement, 1918, when the
electricity failed and the ceremony was held by candlelight, 'the
guns of the War of Independence going off outside', the day the
newly extended Adelaide Road synagogue was reconsecrated in
June 1925 and a celebration held in a marquee by the canal
afterwards, 'all the dignitaries among the Jews there, justices in
the new Irish state, businessmen; famous actresses and
authoresses all in their finery on the gorgeous sunny day'.
Lucien was born an exile. In Dun Laoghaire. His family had
exiled themselves from the Jews around South Circular Road,
the focus of Jewish population in Dublin, where the family had
lived since the 1880s. There was a crockery factory under the
Wicklow mountains, not far from Dun Laoghaire, and the
family moved nearer to it. But there was also the wish to
associate themselves with the most middle-class and secular
environment in Ireland. But links were forcibly kept up and

4

Lucien was eventually sent to the Zion Schools near Kelly's Corner, a marathon bus journey to be undertaken each morning and each afternoon. When he tired of that or his family tired of the effort of pushing him on his journey each morning they settled for a local primary school for him. That was the beginning of a more irrevocable exile for him.

Lucien was born in December 1932. That something terrible was happening to the Jews in Germany he was made aware of in gossipy gatherings of boys in school costumes at street corners around the archetypal corner, Kelly's Corner, boys who were as equally concerned with removing navy chocolate wrappers as they were with the fate of the Jews in Germany. Dublin in those years was a city of solitarily squirting rain clouds and of navy chocolate papers. Then it became a city of girls in navy convent uniforms. These girls had been whipped up by demagogues of Reverend Mothers into applause for fascist leaders, the saviours of the church against the Bolsheviks. Such was the hatred of one of these leaders, for the Jews, that he sent a plane to destroy the Jews of Dublin in January 1941. On the night of 1 January 1941 Greenville Hall Synagogue, on the South Circular Road, was half destroyed by a German bomber and the house of the second reader of the Adelaide Road Synagogue, who lived opposite the Greenville Hall Synagogue, totally destroyed. But no Jews in Dublin were killed. Greenville Hall Synagogue was reopened in September 1941 and Lucien was present.

Nights in London, his daughter making love in the house to a boyfriend, Lucien reconstructed another part of his family legend. This was the most extraordinary part and it was relevant to those war years, Dublin Jews with their own private war against a mass outbreak of anti-Semitism in Irish society. 'They're jealous of us,' his father would always say, 'Jealous of our positiveness, our love of life.' This part of the family history was verified by an excavating Hoagman. The son of Magiash Hoagman, who'd left Dublin shortly after the family arrival in Ireland in the middle of the nineteenth century, had relinquished his Jewishness and become a Hogan, descendants running a butchering business in County Westmeath and fervent Catholics too. Their Jewishness had been totally oblivionized way back. It was not uncommon in Ireland for people to forget their recent heritage seeing that so many of the Irish middle class were survivors of quite recent famine or people who'd managed to cope after evictions from land. Irish family memory in general could not afford to go back very far. So the Hogans in Westmeath were really Jews who'd come to Dublin in the late 1840s. The very blackness of the hair of the Hogan girls could have made you suspicious. They were members of the Blue-shirts, the Irish fascist organization, in the 1930s, their throng dotting the shores of Lake Derravaragh – legendary home of the Children of Lir, royal Irish children haplessly turned into swans, for three hundred years – for picnics. In 1941 Mr Hogan at an open-air wedding table, his black-haired daughters also at the table, made a speech saying that Ireland should do as Germany did and drive the Jews, 'those who'd crucified Our Lord', out. The speech was just one extension of the crazed Catholic triumphalism which gripped Ireland in those times. An excavating Hoagman confronted his relatives, and then rushed back to his business as picture-house owner in Dublin, not having, as he said himself, 'let the cat out of the bag'. But the Dublin Hoagmans could afford to be sly. They were rich, erudite and worldly people now, scoffing at the mores of the country around them and wearing laconic middle-class Dublin brogues. They were loved, despite the prevailing anti-Semitism in Dublin, for their laughter, their smiles and the way their eyes always seemed cocked in a joke. Uncle Adolphe, the picture-house owner, was the most loved one of all and he took on management of a theatre in which there was a pantomime each year until his death.

It was the influence of that uncle which played such a large part in Lucien's plans.

After leaving St Columba's College Rathfarnham in 1951, a Protestant secondary school founded so that landowners could address their tenants in Gaelic, Lucien entered Trinity College. There he befriended Ethel Bannion, a Catholic girl from Limerick, and spent two or three years going to plays with her and discussing the mainstreams of philosophy of the time with her. She was an eager, lonely girl, freckles like oatflakes on her face, eyes that startled out as from a statue of the Virgin Mary, auburn, even coppery curls in her hair. She followed him wherever he went; she was wafted by him. When he took lead parts in college plays she stared at him idolatrously. But when Libby Lazurus came along he fell carnally in love with her and made love for the first time. Libby, a Cork Jewess, came to Trinity in 1954. Hair black as Clonbrassil Street black puddings, eyes that were biblical, exotically alive. He made love to this girl, three years his junior, all over Dublin, in Killiney, Dalkey, in the wastes between Rock Road and the sea, on the top of the Dublin mountains, one day in a field in the Dublin mountains for Sunday picnickers to see. She was sexually carnivorous. She was unashamed. She was the most resplendent girl in Dublin. Then abruptly she threw in Trinity and left Dublin in the autumn of 1955 to go to an acting school. That threw him back on Ethel Bannion. He did not know how to make love to a girl after Libby Lazurus.

Lucien began working as an actor in Dublin in 1956. The world of Uncle Adolphe had exerted its influence over him. But he still had the safety of a university degree. Ethel Bannion was working as a secretary in a law firm, having failed all her way through college since Lucien began having the affair with Libby Lazurus. But still she saw him now and attended the theatre with him and watched him in rehearsal for the plays in which he performed. But there was something more subdued about her. She'd left college without a degree, having given up on it. And occasionally beside Lucien in the theatre seats, during a rehearsal for a play he was in, she came out with a rancorous remark under her breath. But still he tolerated her. The days were greyer in Dublin. The time was greyer. And then one day, beside a travel poster showing Chartres Cathedral at the juncture of Westmoreland Street and D'Olier Street, he saw Libby Lazurus. She was back. He was now twenty-five. She was performing in a pantomime that Christmas in his uncle's theatre. And he began having an affair with her again, as passionately and as mindlessly as before.

It was 1958. He turned twenty-six that December. On the night of his birthday Libby allowed him to make love to her under a bush on the cold ground in St Stephen's Green, the two of them, like winos, having skirted the railings. But there was a backlog of experience Lucien had not coped with. He'd tried to make love to other girls since Libby went and failed. Somehow the armoury of his body didn't work with anyone else, such had been the intensity of what had happened between him and Libby. Word quickly gets around Dublin and it was this word that killed the revival of his relationship with Libby. Full of masculinity, at a New Year's party, 1959, he was suddenly confronted by Ethel Bannion. Immediately he caught sight of her he knew there would be trouble. She approached him, an almost tangible smell of disuse off her. 'You're incapable. Incapable of physical relations with anyone except Libby Lazurus.' He was wearing a white jersey. He stopped dead. 'You're a Jewish lesbian. You can't get it up. You're a sexual failure. A wimp. Come on, show us what a circumcized prick that doesn't work looks like.' Her face, drunk, was an aurora borealis of bitterness. The skin of her face like heaps and heaps of dead porridge. This was her moment. Her speech. Then she withdrew. He couldn't believe it. This was the Third Reich, the Tsarist oppressions manifesting themselves at a Dublin theatrical party where, if the revellers were not actors, they were ex-Trinity students. There was silence. Ethel had made her impact.

He could not make love to Libby after that. In Ethel Bannion's words he could not 'get it up'. She had destroyed something in him. Not just his sexuality, but his belief in the steadiness of human nature. He lost his innocence the night Ethel had attacked him. Shortly after that, his ignominy with Libby and her quick withdrawal from him, he left Ireland.

Yes, he gave up his pretensions to the theatre about the same time. Was it a coincidence? Anyway he'd married the daughter of a failed, rural Tory parliamentary candidate a few years later. She'd brought him back to sexual life; she'd conquered, by her quietness, the deadness in him. He was working for an insurance company in the city by then and extravagantly successful at what he has doing. 'The righteous shall flourish like the palm tree: he shall grow like a cedar in Lebanon.'

8

In the late 1970s he had occasion to visit Beirut for business reasons. He stood on a street in this city with evening hitting a few high-rise buildings with a sun which was a perfect orange and thought: nothing in this city, for all its carnage, can be worse than what Ireland tried to do to me; it tried systematically to take the flesh from the bone; it tried to eliminate me. He stood, perilously still, a professional briefcase in his right hand.

By then, of course, Ireland was just a memory. His father died in 1967. The burial was nostalgically Jewish. Clay from a black desert in the Wicklow mountains under his head, his head tentatively turned to the east – the verge of the Hill of Howth on the opposite side of the bay. Lucien recited the Hebrew prayers at Dolphin's Barn Jewish Cemetery among a gaggle of half-embarrassed men in heavy, charcoal coats. His father had always lit two candles on Friday evenings in Dun Laoghaire so that often the candles were reflected on the image of the sea; his father had inserted the Scrolls of the Law back into the Ark of the Covenant in Adelaide Road Synagogue; his father had led the Jews of Dublin out of the old year often as the Bridegroom of the Torah and brought them back to Lebanon Lodge for festivities.

Lucien watched the silver bells tinkle on the Scrolls of the Law the following Saturday in Adelaide Road Synagogue as he would have as a child. But more than years separated him from then. He was not really his father's son. He was not an heir. He wanted to get away quickly from brothers who were forcing familial obligations on him. He didn't want any of these arabesques. When his mother died the house was sold and the money portioned among the family. There was no house in Ireland now for him to bring his children back to. But still it haunted him, Lebanon Lodge, a house become more ghostly with the years. It was the house of the dead. Ironic that Ethel Bannion, now grown fat, had married a member of the ruling party in the Irish parliament, another parliamentary representative of the same party having purchased the house. But political parties come and go, especially in Ireland. Irish politics as everyone knows are quixotic. But the house in Lucien's mind had a steadiness, a ghostly permanence. It lived in a world of night in Maida Vale. His relationship with his brothers was, as it had always been, negligible. They were Dublin businessmen, intent on keeping the idea of family up. He had an English accent now. The Irish connections had come to nothing. One of his brothers kept the factory going and another hovered around it. They were forever making overtures to him, those overtures having begun as soon as he had thrown in the theatre for business. But he suspected them. He had done with them. Yet something nagged him. About Ireland. About his youth there. He entered the front door of Lebanon Lodge in his dreams and the whole of a history of a Jewish family revealed itself to him, a history since their arrival in Ireland. They had married Jewish history with Irish history and made a covenant out of which he'd been born. He'd been the Jewish boy who'd vacantly written an essay entitled 'A house tells its story' in a Christian Brothers school in Dun Laoghaire. He fidgeted with the pen again in his mind and put the last strokes on the essay. It was the 1980s and his children were grown. His daughter worked in the theatre. She brought theatrical friends to his party on Christmas night in Maida Vale each year. Girls with short dresses and striped woollen stockings. Striped marionettes in Southern Bohemia? By default they'd become a kind of aristocracy. The children of the rich came to the party. Fenella, the heiress, of the long legs in the brief dress and of the little mirthful fountain of a head. Even the daughter, herself Jewish, of a man who made long and boring speeches in the Houses of Parliament, a girl with salient, tangerine lips. But for some reason he had to admit that his children, for all their easy artistic pursuits, were somewhat boring to him. They were beyond a border of understanding. Try as hard as they could they'd never be able to go back on that border. They were somewhat soulless, like their friends. People complimented him at the party for being so young-looking, as young-looking as his sons, his dark hair still shining and his skin pristine, that skin that had been married to Libby Lazurus's radiating skin once in a moment of total forgetfulness. But his lingering youthfulness made him oddly alone-looking there, standing among the hubbub of a Christmas night party in Maida Vale as he had stood on a street in Lebanon when the sun was going down and the high-rise buildings were aflame with meteors of colour, the tokens of the tired sun on them, and his mind had been shot through with an awareness of how close to extinction he'd come, whether extinction in Dublin during the war when the Germans were thinking of invading or extinction at a theatrical party in Dublin, not far from Kelly's Corner, when a woman had breathed her own brand of genocide into his body.

Elysium

It is nearly ten years now since I arrived in London. It is a long and involved story as to how I came here. I married at eighteen. I was, literally, a product of the bogs, but our bogs were close to, hugged Pontoon Ballroom in County Mayo. So from as early as fourteen years of age I was stealing over the bogs on a bicycle and creeping into the ballroom with older sisters. I presented myself, talcumed, usually in pale blue, a ribbon on; a piece of bog cotton, a flower from the meadows, a rapt fluff of cloud. The men of Ireland looked me up and down. And I began to dance. My teenage years were ones of dancing and giving myself. I think it was my red ribbon which attracted attention to me first but the men always went for me. So there was a price on me. I got a lot of icecreams out of it in Castlebar. My body became worn very quickly because of it, my face became brazen, my tongue unsalacious as I licked icecream bowls. I was ostracized among my sisters; my success had swept them out of the scene. But there was Achill Island and bays I was brought to in the summer. In short to the men of Mayo I was a 'good thing'.

I slept uneasily on my sexual abandon. I had dreams of future catastrophes because of it. Nearby Our Lady of Knock appeared and she rummaged with my dreams. With St John and sometimes St Joseph she poked at me with a shepherd's stick and like a nun at school told me – in a broad Mayo accent – 'to cop on'. As with nuns at school I refused her. I gave more of myself. My body turned from white to pink. I was eighteen and I met my man then. He owned a garage in the countryside near Castlebar. 'The Sheriff', he was called. He went around in American country and western apparel, big boots on him, a cowboy hat, valentine hearts embroidered into his shirt and his crotch always in evidence. I was 'his gal', he told me. He had lots of money, a garage in the countryside constantly attacked and mediated over by wild geese. We danced in Pontoon Ballroom for three months before marrying. My mother stood outside the cottage as he made off with me to our new home, a suburban house outside Castlebar. She had got rid of a handful but she had gained a prosperous son-in-law. I was a wealthy young woman now, all because of my body and my looks I told myself. I took trains to Dublin for hairdos. I wrote country and western songs in my spare time. Country and western songs became poems for me. That was the first sign of discussion. Little bits of poetry by loaves of brown bread in our suburban, blankly lighted kitchen, 'O Lord give me freedom. O Lord give me pain.' What I wanted pain for I was not sure but pain came when the children came, Tomás, Micheál and Tibby – called after an American country and western singer – I had to fight to keep the pure lines in my body and with my physical beauty flawed by childbirth and the idea of lechery ruptured by marriage my husband collected girls in the bogs and brought them off to Achill for weekends, making love to them under a crucifix situated high over the Atlantic.

All this is not telling much about me, my feelings at the time, the woman who walked about the house in country and western boots. I became very lonely. There was a big picture of mountains in our sitting room. I wanted to be buried like Queen Maeve on top of a mountain.

I realized too at that time that I was an exceptional kind of person. I was pretty, had blonde ringleted hair, did what most women in Castlebar could not do, wrote poetry. I recalled moments in childhood I'd heard voices in my dreams telling me to go to remote hills in the bog to receive messages from God. Maybe I'd missed what I should have been, a virgin, always a virgin, not a nun but a woman who drifts around the town declaring her virginity like a no man's land in war, a place of pain and thoughts and feelings too much to accommodate on any side.

I was curtailed, though, during these conjectures by memories of tender caresses from a young boy in a bog; Castlebar faced me, the mountains, the sea, years of suburban houses and masses of adulteries. The money was pouring in. My husband talked of holidays in Spain. It was summer and girls outside icecream parlours slouched, looking at me knowingly. A boy from Sweden passed the men's lavatory, a rucksack caked on his back. The girls were ones who travelled to remote corners with my husband. I was the wife, the mother. There were landslides within me; I walked as erect as possible, how a nun at school had ordained one should walk erect. Without the children – they had become bold, whingeing and brattish now – I found a rubbish dump on a beach by which I walked along, the sluice gates of sewers opening on to the beach and gulls diving down to question old, blackened contorted kettles. There was a face forming within me. It was a boy's face. I created a boy I wanted to get to know, not sexually, not anything like that. There was a photograph missing from inside me that should have been taken. I created, I invented an area; I wanted to conquer that area. I knew I would not find this boy in Castlebar but I was also sure he existed somewhere; there was the map of these finer things in me, the shape of a green squelching map of Ireland on the wall at school. I wanted a word to set me off wandering; I thought of fleeing with the tinkers once or twice. Matt, the husband, smelled of semen. But the more I walked by a rubbish dump, the higher the ecstasy, the more suffocating the knowledge that I was trapped. There must have been thousands of Irish women in my position I thought, millions of women. I did not intend to start the women's lib movement in Castlebar. Instead I wove wings of fancy. But they refused to fly very far. So I kept my eye on the shop in which I could buy tickets to England.

'Dear whoever you are, I went because – because I could not stand it any more. I could not stand being a lump of – I don't want to use a rude word. I went to try to salvage my most ancient dignity.' Words, notes were played with. I needed an excuse. By this time marriage, a husband, did not exist. He took a girl back home one day and made love to her on the couch. I smelt it, under the picture of Connemara mountains. This was

14

just one of the incidents that slid into the sequence of going. I did not know what I was saying goodbye to when I purchased fresh emerald boat tickets to England in a shop in Castlebar in October for myself and my children. I'm sorry I cannot give you a dramatic incident which preceded my going; in fact between the first leaves of autumn and a boat journey to England there is only a blur, a blur on which is written a kind of Sanskrit. 'I am Mary Mullarney, twenty-four. I possess three yellow ochre cardigans and three children.' That month, in London, my life began, however dazed and erratic was its beginning.

London, refuge of sinners, of lost Irishwomen; its chief import is people from my part of Mayo. I often feel like addressing it; it is not England, it is not in the demesne of the queen; it is an invented place. But a place which also dulls one, especially one who can hardly remember her former life.

'Piss off.' I had a sister in Harrow, 41 Bengeworth Road. I understood I could approach at her door. I was mistaken. She was married now to an Englishman who drove trucks to Aberdeen – she'd converted him to Catholicism – and the Harrow church hall was nearby. On this wall were photographs of herself among church committees. She was the one who when I was fourteen most hated me. I'd broken some rule of the dance-hall floor. I'd appeared in a blue taffetta-effect dress once. There were certain dresses you could wear and certain dresses you couldn't. She'd never forgiven me and one night – when her husband was probably plunging into beans at a motorway stop near Easingwold – she slammed a door on me and Tomás, Micheál and Tibby in Harrow. Not before I'd noticed mathematical problems of lines and contortions on her face. She'd have to see Father-some-thing-or-another in the morning to discuss the serving of coffee at the next meeting of the Mayo hurlers' association. The odd thing about families is that they're illusions. Far from being the closest to you they're very often the most diabolical of people. There were no icecream parlours open in Harrow and Micheál, Tomás, Tibby and myself ended up in Westbourne Park later one night or early one morning. We had our bags, our rugs, I had my savings and we celebrated. It was a black perky girl who brought us to 'Elysium'.

'Elysium' was chalked in white on the right-hand column of a gate outside a generously decaying Edwardian house on a starlit night. Lenny, a scarlet ribbon in the laced strands of hair tied above her head, led us up the path. Tomás clashed against a dustbin and I bid him hush. I was entering a house in the fields of Mayo. The night was dark among the stone walls. I trod tentatively on the door step. The occupants were gone; to America, wherever. This house had a secret for me. It was after a dance. A door opened in a house in Mayo on to a house in London. There was a cooker, a fridge, heaters, bedding, everything we needed. The house was deserted, Lenny said, but for an Irish boy who never emerged from his room. Then she disappeared. After poking around a bit we lay down among Foxford blankets.

Great trouble had visited this house; the people were rich; the girls wore red tartan skirts. One of the girls became pregnant, tried to abort the baby among the streams which constantly cleansed the fluff of sheep, the red of her blood had run with the brook – a sign – and the whole family had left for America. But the boy. The father. I could see him against a half-door.

Raymond was from Belfast. I pulled back the door on him. He had a face, frail and white as Easter lilies against the Edwardian light of the window. Squatting on the floor, he was reading a poem by George Herbert out loud. 'Love bade me welcome; yet my soul drew me back. Guilty of dust and sin.' I was heading for the shutters which were not quite open. 'Isn't it time you were up having your breakfast. Hello there, I'm Mary. Yes I know all about you. No need for introductions. We've moved in. We'll make a nice household. So you're from the Red Hand of Ulster. Sweet Jesus you don't look like an Ulsterman. Come up and meet the children. The tea's made. How many sugars do you take? I was now at the window, looking outside, my hands grabbing the worn-away cream of the shutters as the visions outside petrified me.

Already Cormac Fitzmaurice from Dublin was up, a large bottle of Guinness sprouting from his black maggoty coat picked up from a rubbish dump – among the florets of used durexes and among the heroin syringes – shouting as he eddied to and fro about Synge Street Christian Brothers' school and one brother who used to ride a pie-bald pony, bare back, on Sandymount Strand at dawn. Behind him the graffiti on the pub opposite was choice. 'Come to Ballinacargy for pimples on your prick.'

Raymond struggled free from his Buddha position and quickly came to breakfast with me and the children. White shirt rolled up on his thin arms he charmed the children; Micheál, Tomás and Tibby smiled gratefully at him. It was the first time really I realized I had children, not little piglets. I counted the freckles on Micheál's nose that morning.

'I was born in a red brick part of a red brick city. There were hills and mountains around the city. My ma inherited a newsagent's from her dad. The *Irish Independent* was advertised outside. The front was whiney green. We were taigues. My dad was jealous of my mother's shop and tried to burn it down one night. He worked at the station and shuffled along to work in the mornings under low mountains. At the local public baths Catholic and Protestant children swam. At the age of four I was nearly drowned by a Protestant boy of six who looked like a ferocious gorilla.'

I washed Raymond's shirts, often dots of darker white on them. 'Made in Italy' frequently boasted on the collar tag. Threads of blood disappeared into the water in the big, white, bath-like sink. I scrubbed inches of collar dirt on a wash board. The material was occasionally silk and pleasant to deal with. White shirts hung up in the kitchen like angels.

'Growing up in a city where blood has collected under the houses you have mischievous aunts and uncles. They canonize soldiers. There are wreaths around the pictures in their sitting rooms. Aunts and uncles sit like officers. They command imaginary armies. In another part of the city are other children whose aunts and uncles command different imaginary armies. One uncle of mine had a picture of Patrick Pearse in a frame and because there was no glass on it – they were too poor – Patrick Pearse's mouth was once stubbed away by a cigarette butt. He looked like Dracula then. Draculas sold Easter lilies outside the public baths. When I was fourteen Protestant children no longer swam at the public baths.'

In newly washed white shirts Raymond looked like a different person. I washed his hair one night over the kitchen sink and Tibby – aged three – dried it. The kitchen smelt of lavender then. I realized that night my husband or the black-garbed nuns had not come looking for us. We were the queen's property now. We had found another country.

'The first time you see death is the worst. I saw a child: its brains blown out. I thought of all the poems by Patrick Pearse blown to nothing. It was a Protestant bomb. You could always tell Protestant bombs because it was always children who seemed to be caught in them. Protestant Gods were different from Catholic Gods; they lived in houses of dark stone and punished children who carried rosary beads in their pockets.'

Raymond in a white silk shirt, rolled up, stripes of primrose and thrush hair on his shoulders, a cigarette in his fingers, he talking, his lips the colour of lips that have just been moistened by wine. That's one of the photographs taken in my mind at the kitchen table in November.

'Then came the real armies. In a city where the houses were armies, the eyes of houses in the hills, to encounter the real armies was to meet a ghost. Faces were painted out. It was all part of a logic; the grave too was part of a logic. Wreaths were wrapped in newspaper that would otherwise have held fish and chips and placed together with the news of local commandants in the paper, by wet grave slabs in Milltown cemetery. I remember one wreath of flowers, little pink and red flowers, miniature flowers, almost plastic flowers. It was a woman with a scarf on her head who laid this wreath for her son, a school friend of mine. We were given berets and flags to compensate for the dead.'

Once or twice I pulled Raymond up, asking him what he meant by something or another and that stopped him really, so to fill in the gap, his white shirt catching the gleams of a candle we considered appropriate for the occasion, I mustered everything I had and took off where he stopped, in a mustard cardigan, arms folded, telling my life story as I concentrated on a pound of butter which had slipped into the shape of Croagh Patrick on the table.

'Where do I begin? Let's see. Let me rack my brains. Brown bogs. Creaking, spinning bicycles. Milk churns. Girls were solicitous about scapulars. Geese were coy. I shared a secret with the heavens. I was to be sainted one day. Girls rummaged through bogs. Girls were friends until men came along. Girls stooped and lacquered their shoes with rival cream. There was a picture of Marie Goretti in our sitting room among millions of sea-shells and small pigeon feathers glued on the wall, and despite the fact that she was sainted for resisting the advances of a man, girls in newly laundered dresses and with new hairdos, before going to dances, fell on their knees in front of her and hands raised high in prayer begged her not to allow them to be shipwrecked in the jostle for a good man on the ballroom floor of their fledgling years.'

Funerals at first seemed to be the only point of contact between my discourses and Raymond's; hearses galloping through the brown marshes of Mayo, hearses, piled with their fill of flowers, languishing through Belfast. But the point of contact widened to an abstract and unstated notion which united us. This house was like the Irish flag. It brought a part of the green and a part of the gold together. It was the peaceable white between. I'd never before spoken at length with someone from the other part of my island. This city with its sleeping November dustbins afforded me the opportunity to do just that. This house was like a cavern of lost history lessons; nuns squawked with news of imminent invasions. In my dreams Raymond kept coming towards me. He came out of the white of the Irish flag. Reflections of water rippling on his face. Cowslips somewhere in the vicinity and the winnowing of the Irish flag sometimes wringing the sound of classical music. He came out of the tender things of my childhood. Like the fluttering of the flag he was caught in the act of motion; the expectation of his arrival was never met by his arrival. He was a part of me caught for years in the act of approaching and with all the attendant vagueness of line that entailed.

'A lad brought me out of a dance one moonlit night and confessed to me his ambition was to be a missionary priest in a Central American republic where the people would have to come to him for advice about revolution and sewers but first he had to do you know what with a young lady. So he asked me if I'd oblige him and lift my skirt. I said "No thanks Father", slapped his face, pushed him into a moonlit brook and wished him luck with the holy revolutions in South America.'

London was the lifting of a weight; it was shuffling the Concise Oxford Dictionary at Maida Vale library; it was acquainting myself with the linear lonely hearts columns; it was paying a visit to a family planning clinic and having something stuck in me. There I baulked. I returned to 'Elysium' and in the tradition of my mother baked a loaf of brown bread and kept repeating a phrase I concocted for Raymond a few nights previously: 'No white stale bread here as in Central America, Father. No white stale bread here as in Central America, Father.'

Gulls lolled over the grey Edwardian houses as if waiting for white bread. They got graffiti. Some of the graffiti was by my fellow countrymen. 'Life to those who understand and fuck the begrudgers.' My own language had become less auspicious. Black girls were trapped in red telephone kiosks. My children had improvised a see-saw among the syringes outside and I ordered them in once or twice. But there was more than just the grey outside to rescue them from. A creature halfway between the bygone hippie and the punk who was to come a few years later pulled himself along; the backs of Afghan coats had become lathery and polemical ex-public-school boys enlivened the world of Marx with candy-pink shoes. But confronting the grey outside one day I knew I could easily accommodate myself to it and all its ensuing threats; 'for better or for worse' as a green-toothed priest had spat at my white, backswept crown of a veil once – it was to be home.

'Dear Aunt Bethan. I'm living in London now. It's a very grey city but there's also warmth here. You would not expect it at first arriving at Euston Station but it grows on you. It's like lifting a dustbin lid and finding salmon instead of chewed-away kippers. I live in a fine big house. In fact it's not unlike yours. I bought a brooch for you at Portobello market last Friday. I'll keep it to send later as I want to post this now and I'd have to wrap the brooch up. Tibby has taken all the tissue. The children are grand; Micheál and Tomás are going to school. They learn about worms that enter your bloodstream if you bathe in African rivers which they never learnt at home. I hope you are well. Remember what you once said to me: "One good lace blouse can be worth more than a marriage." '

When I went to post that letter the mail-box refused to accept it. Aunt Bethan was a spinster aunt who lived alone in a big house by the river outside Ballina. She was the only one of my relatives I liked. As a child I'd been fascinated by the silver pointed pins in her pouch-like grey velvet hats.

'Why did I leave Belfast? You've got to leave haven't you? It's one of the laps along the way. What am I going to do now? Don't know. O yes.' Raymond was going to say something but stopped. 'Red brick cottages building into a palace. That's the dream. My father used always to want to eat cornflakes on Coney Island. It was a name that stuck in his head. Me?' Raymond shrugged. 'The funny thing about red brick cottages under low mountains is that they kill me's.'

My children brought bread and honey to the genii in the lower room as offerings. We visited London zoo; we visited big stores in which premature santas had already made an appearance. But Raymond dominated. He never went out. He'd come with the house. He just sat surrounded by books and devouring their contents like a rat. Once or twice in the café of a big department store, a red tartan skirt on me, in sudden exultation I imagined, as in a Hollywood movie, Raymond, the other side of the table, clenching the white and tender part of my wrists mouthing some sublimity that made everyone in the café perk up and listen, his hair falling, a blond fluency – the colour of Raymond's hair fluctuated from dark to fair. But of course he never ventured out to make such a scene real. I'm sure he would have clenched my wrists like that had he come out. Not in any romantic way. We were friends now. Mates.

A gull spiralled into the air above our mansions, a festive eddying of a white uprising streamer. The gull climbed to a point where he could see all London. I had a part-time job now and Raymond when I went out looked after the children.

Raymond did go out. He came with us on our second visit to

London zoo. He wore a crocheted hat over his ears – one of mine – and he pointed to a polar bear on a grey November day and said that he'd always wanted a nose like a polar bear's, a nose that was so solemn and pacific.

I could not fully cope with our relationship on the level of the real so I created the fantastic; anyway our relationship always had buried in it an element of fantasy. I was the girl in the red tartan skirt in the house; he kept coming towards me. I was off to America. The smell of pristine new land, its riverside firs and its sluggish, congenial rivers already in my nostrils. But I was being separated from the boy I loved. For some reason there were always a dozen kegs of beer in the kitchen beside me so the smell of porter invaded the smells of the fir trees and unhurried waters. Raymond was always in white. That was his colour. And his hair was white. My arms were always waiting but he was entranced in a slow, continually revolving motion. I'd woken once or twice to find tears on my rich and ornate Foxford rug.

The winos up the road burned their house down. They came running out in the middle of the night, tails of their coats on fire but bottles of Guinness still outheld. Cormac Fitzmaurice was seen to be waltzing with a hot water jar on the opposite pavement, gurgling to his dancing partner that it was he who'd started the fire. As if to validate his Nero claims his cheeks were smudged in red lipstick and red lipstick daubed his lips. There were red smears on the hot water jar. But Rome did not burn down that night. Just the house. As he danced Cormac had a litre bottle of whiskey sticking out of his pocket. The label had messages scribbled in red biro on it. A woman with a youngish face, her hair white as a bog cotton under a mauve chiffon scarf, her hands deep in the pockets of her plush whitish coat, then began screaming, affirmedly facing the house, that she was the culprit. A competition ensued between her and Cormac, who'd stopped dancing, the two of them looking at the burning house, Cormac revealing that he'd loved setting houses on fire since he was a child and he'd once incinerated alive an aunt and her two trimmed white poodles in her house in Blackrock, County Dublin. The children claimed they saw three burning rats perched on the roof of that house against the multiple stars and frenzied sparks that night.

A bomb went off in England. It tore through the entrails of the media. Many young people were killed. It ruptured the bowels of consciousness. We picked our way in a different planet for a few weeks. A Pakistani girl at school prodded Micheál's bum with a compass and venomously informed him he was a murdering Paddy and should return to where he came from. I maintained queenly dignity at work – gracefully mopping floors – bald managers stooped towards me. Well it wasn't me who planted the bomb. What about the beam in your own eye? But the structure of my house was impaired. The landscape of England was transformed. Biting winds were said to have crept down motorways and isolated motorway cafés. A hideous orange light had overtaken everything. It glared in at night. Escaping it I descended to the cellars to try to discover the truth.

'The English invaded Ireland in the twelfth century and they've been a bloody nuisance ever since. They ruined the crops and ransacked convents.' An elderly, fragile nun at school contorted during history lessons. 'Mind you there were some decent Protestants. Theobald Wolfe Tone being one such. To him is the credit of the Irish flag, green, white and gold. Green for Catholic. Gold for Orangeman. White for a true and lasting peace between.' The only orange I saw was the orange of the light outside; it even changed the colour of Raymond's white dotted shirt as he crouched sacrosanctly on the floor. 'Let us all pray girls for a United Ireland.' Theobald Wolfe Tone slouched along Sutherland Avenue in an old manky coat, a newspaper cutting dripping from his pocket.

'My mother did not love my father but she married him. My father did not love my mother but he married her. My mother loved me but I was kidnapped by uncles with republican eyes. The annual Wolfe Tone commemoration was a great event. My uncles would get drunk in a nearby pub and start pissing on the other graves. That was the great festive point of the year. Pissing on graves in the cemetery Wolfe Tone was buried in. There was a little bridge over a brook nearby and in a short blue coat I'd run off there. I met a cow there once and we performed a pantomime together while the Wolfe Tone commemoration speeches were being made.'

The odd thing about Raymond was that since this bombing his load had lightened a bit; he'd begun telling foul jokes, he quoted poetry freely. The children loved his telling of stories. He'd got them from a grandmother who lived in a house in the Antrim mountains, he told them.

'My grandmother was Scottish really. She had boots in her voice, black boots. Children we gathered. Her stories were of ghouls and headless men. She emphasized the blood around the rings of the headless men's necks. As a girl she'd been lifted to and fro on gentle waves by currachs. She was in a different land now and rewarded the natives with monstrosities.'

Where Raymond's granny came from there was a church; a Catholic church. The faith had been preserved there but the statues were unusually bloody. Christs with blood streaming from their wounds, Marys with blood congealed at their hearts and in their heavenward gazing eyes. Always a story of moving from one place to another, the currachs on gentle waves eventually bringing them to waves of a more turbulent kind.

'There was a giant who lived in a castle on the edge of black bog.' I became one of the children. I listlessly filed in for Raymond's story. Raymond's granny had made many shirts, embroidered them, so I bought a white shirt, and embroidered it blue for Raymond's birthday. A new shirt. A new human being. We dipped into wine and sang. December the tenth. It was drawing towards Christmas. I didn't send any Christmas cards to Ireland.

Raymond in an off-white embroidered shirt, serious creases in the shirt; his birthday. I had cut his hair, it had solemnized his head; candlelight caught and fiddled with gold locks. Raymond looked out – beyond the swooning candles what did he see? Mexico, Italy, Morocco. It was a time for currachs again but this time currachs would land in uncustomary blue waters.

My children looked as students put up barricades. The state was coming. Charred beams stuck out where the wino's house had been. The battering of hammers went on through the night. The local population of prostitutes, students, heroin merchants was threatened with eviction. The house I shared with Raymond was the only one without barricades. The state was welcome. We knew all about the state.

'Blood, blood in the gutters, blood on white-washed house fronts. Blood on an old lady's handbag. She looked at her bag with sudden disapproval as if the only appropriate thing was that it should fly away. The blood encircled her feet. It eddied under her. She started to scream and then I tried to scream and I couldn't and I woke and I found a rat peering out a hole with much curiosity at me.' Raymond was rambling. There was still an odd quiet hammer going. I'd brought him cocoa. I'd brought it right to his lips. A candle threw panoramic shadows in an Edwardian room. I'd had dreams like that as a girl in Mayo. I'd woken, gone to a window, tried to throw myself out. There seemed no returning from a state of madness. You had broken forever with the laws of logic. The laws that govern and make up everyday living. You had crossed some border into a hell. I suddenly looked into Raymond's pale blue eyes – they were the same colour as the walls in parts of this house – and saw he had broken forever with the logic that governs everyday living and sustains even the vaguest cohesion of a will for everyday survival.

Micheál, hands behind his back, in a short blue coat, on a black and white day stood beside the charred beams of the winos' house; I went out to retrieve him from a photograph of Leningrad after the siege I'd seen in a book in Maida Vale library.

'Something's drumming in my head. Something's beating it in. I don't own it any more. It's not mine. Once when I felt like this I used think of my granny as a girl in a red tartan skirt – she kept evil away – but it doesn't work any more. I'll have to think of something different. I can't. I'll think of you Mary.'

Mary was preparing for Christmas; she was travelling to the perimeter of her mind, shores in west Mayo where mountains were hidden in the evening reflections. Mary in a yellow ochre cardigan began to say a kind of prayer, a prayer different from the ones she was taught. She said prayers for her children, for Raymond. She grappled again for words that were sacred as a

25

child. London revived the glint of evening on mother-of-pearl beads. She found things she thought she had lost forever; it was advent in London and mistletoe was brought for rides on the Circle line. A black man holding mistletoe opposite her as the tube was drawing towards Westbourne Park told her to cheer up, that Christmas was coming. She looked at him. She had not been doleful. She'd been thinking of anterooms of her existence darkened for years and now lighted by a strange and probing grey light.

Raymond became nervous, shivering. He carried trays about him with teapots on them. He began to act like a manservant, bringing tea to me as I lay in bed on Saturday mornings – the bed had been transported in from a skip by four friendly West Indians. 'Leave it there,' I'd ordered him. Then I'd search out his face. Every day I looked into it I saw something new crashing in it.

'I wanted to say something. I wanted to tell you something. But I couldn't find the words. Words are strange aren't they? They've declared a war on my words. They've tried to take my vocabulary from me.'

The state did not come. The state did not show much interest as yet in the decrepit houses. Students hitched home for Christmas. Prostitutes put their legs up and watched their little yelping TVs.

'I wanted to tell you something. I wanted to tell you something. I wanted to tell you something.' Raymond managed to scream one night but when I tried to put my arms about him he began shuddering; he did not want me to hold him.

Why wasn't he hitching home for Christmas? Why was I devoting so much time to him? I started becoming annoyed with the idea of him. There were some days I wanted to shake him but I was restrained by the presence of a dream: a boy in white and a girl in a red tartan skirt. This house was one I'd visited before. I was familiar with its rooms as I was familiar with its pain; I had come to relieve some of the pain from its big old walls.

Shortly before Christmas a new woman arrived on the street and she made speeches outside at night about the coming of doom; the judgement; the nuclear bomb. She was from

Wexford. Somehow forebodings of the nuclear bomb got mixed up one night as she stood in the middle of the road with her autobiography. She was a Protestant. Her father was a vicar in Wexford. Someone had given her a large bottle of whiskey for Christmas and she raised it in the air and shouted, 'Does anyone have any holly? I'm itchy.'

I didn't see Raymond much before Christmas. I was working hard. London, its sea of Christmas, swept about me. Nigerian girls sang carols outside St Martin-in-the-Fields. I wanted to stop and thank them but the crowd was too thick and too onward rushing.

Two days before Christmas a boy in white who looked the image of Raymond passed. His face was tanned. He'd obviously been South. He was all in white except for an Afghan coat. He passed a bird who was snipping at a whole packet of white sliced bread thrown out into a dustbin.

'Hello. How are you?' I entered Raymond's room. He was just sitting there, saying nothing. 'Well Merry Christmas.' Christmas was a day off. Raymond did not want to talk and I closed the door, saying, 'We'll all be having turkey tomorrow night.'

I pushed around London that day; I floated on the crowd, I had no more shopping to do but I just wanted to be part of this intimacy. I belonged now, I was a member of this metropolis and I wanted to share with the crowd the day before Christmas.

Where do Cormac Fitzmaurices and drunk vicars' daughters go for Christmas? There was no one on the street that night. Just a youth passed. A pink chiffon scarf around his neck and his hands enveloped in his pockets and his head worriedly bent over.

I didn't go to midnight mass. With the children I stood at the window and looked in the direction of the church of Our Lady Queen of Heaven in Queensway. I knew I would not be going home again, except for their funerals, not for their marriages. 'Leave father, mother, sisters, brothers, and come follow me.' The half-remembered text of Christ in my mind. I had crossed a border now. There was no going back. My appearance had changed. My face had changed. I had no need of mother or father or sisters or brothers. Or husband. They'd tried to do me in. This city, this unkind sprawl, had given me back a modicum of self-respect and had pointed me on a road again. In the middle of the family planning clinics and the abortion stopping points Christ was tucked into his crib in a church where winos snoozed and snortled now during midnight canticles.

I'd never been a very extravagant cook but I'd bought the *Times* cookbook and in its pages found the most elaborate Christmas dishes.

Sugar glazed gammon.

Slow roast turkey with chestnut stuffing.

Duchesse potatoes.

Purée of Brussels sprouts.

Apricots with brandy and cream.

Plum pudding with brandy butter.

And something called 'the bishop' on which we all got merry. Hot port with sugar, cloves, lemon and mixed spice.

Raymond in a three-piece dark suit I'd picked up for him hid and spluttered with laughter behind a bottle of Beaujolais nouveau. A fire blazed obligingly. I was wearing a white sleeveless blouse I'd presented to myself for Christmas. Daddy Christmas had abandoned ruminative toys under the Christmas tree. Wooden lorries from Norway. Dolls from Tibet. A reproduction of a Michelangelo print was now tacked uncertainly, on the wall, Christ in the nude, rising. Micheál bawled out a song in the Irish language. Tibby gave us a nursery rhyme in an English accent. Tomás yelled that he wanted more turkey after the final helping of the pudding. In our state of merriment we had party games and party games led to a play Raymond and I did together.

He took off his suit and played me, putting on a dress. I put on his suit. The children loved it. My whole life had been waiting for a play. There'd always been an imminent play. The mass. Ragged, scrawny pageants at school. To perform, to dramatize, the need to do these things, was always in my nature. This was an improvisation. There were no ready-made lines. But the script had been arranged.

Raymond: 'Well now, Mr. What's it your after?'

Me: 'A nice young lady.'

28

Raymond: 'Haven't you found one yet?'

Me: 'I've been looking in all kinds of places. I fell in love with a nun but she up and slipped away when she was in my arms. She left a holy medal though.'

The children howled with laughter. But there was also another play taking place.

I have met you before in another time. This city brings other times, past lives together. I know your face. You're part of a shared guilt. We did it together.

I knew something that night I'd suspected for a long time. It slipped out. Beside Tibby Raymond in worn clothes suddenly began laughing and his laughter became drunken and hysterical and then it became crying and then it became screaming. He allowed me to hold him. He was shivering. He kept saying. 'It wasn't me. It wasn't me.'

Raymond: 'The city was orange. We arrived on an orange night. I'd been coming for years. My uncles had babbled on the journey about Gaelic football and heroes that had scored points in County Down years before. I'd heard all this before. I'd grown up with it. There were many things I tried to do in my life-span to be free of this babble. Read. Tried Art school. Dabbled with self-portraits. But something always drew you into the smoky circle. The funereal voices, the faces contemplating the cards. It was as if there wasn't a you, couldn't be a you until you'd done something terrible to atone for an unknown past. Besides there were rungs on a ladder. Trying to be different wasn't easy. Trying to get out was impossible. We arrived and walked from the boat through the orange lights. My uncles had a slip of paper that was soiled with Guinness and tobacco. It was an address in this city. A woman answered. Her face was a skull in the orange light. I was the one who was going to place the device. In a Derry accent she to me, "Sure you have the face of a ewe."'

An outrage was done in this house once. A young woman separated from a young man. The female part of a person separated from the male. The childhood part of the person separated from the adult. The creative from the social. One part of a country was amputated from another.

Raymond was in my bed when they clambered in. It was six in the morning. I'd been lying awake; Raymond there, turned towards me. His face, his cold white body like a ewe's all right. We had not made love. Just slept together under a large multicoloured tinker's shawl of a Foxford rug. One of the men from the anti-terrorist squad took up a position alongside us. He was squat and gruff. I'd been expecting them. 'Merry Christmas,' I said and one young fellow threw himself against the door, facing us with a revolver.

'Dear Aunt Bethan. I'm nearly ten years in London and there's a lot I want to say to you. The reason I'm writing is because I passed the street the other day. There are brand-new council flats there, regimented ones. Raymond's been in jail now nearly ten years. It wasn't anything like a large bombing he'd been responsible for. A small and almost forgotten one. He writes poetry in prison now and some of his poems appear in Republican papers. They mistake the images of doves as symbols of a struggle for a free Ireland. Needless to say I've polished my accent since. I did a secretarial course and am in quite luxurious employment as a secretary. The council long ago rehoused me and Micheál and Tomás and Tibby. I'm a nice polite middle-class person now. Well almost. Micheál is bigger than I am. He's grown to the ceiling. He teaches me things about ancient Egypt and ancient Greece. Tibby wears tight pink satin jeans. I'm writing really to commemorate and celebrate coming to this city. I've kept my word. I never went back to Ireland. We wait here in our comfortable lodgings for the nuclear bomb, mushroom cloud, whatever, but in the meantime have a good time. There are lots of laughs, lots of celebrations but the laughter is innermost and most intense when I think of him in the corridors of his prison and I think of the cells of his poetry, now like Easter lilies they grow until they fill my mind and I want to appeal to the prime minister or the queen on his behalf, saying it wasn't his fault; it was other people. It was the pre-ordained. There'd been no one around to salvage his sanity at the time. But I know they would not listen to me so instead I try to teach my children what this city taught me: love. Yes, Aunt Bethan, love will bring us through the night of the nuclear bomb and the onset of middle age. It will bring us through the nights when the children and the people have gone. There was a night of accord once, a night of simplicity and that makes up for an awful lot, doesn't it?'

The Tipperary Fanale

Olivieri Di Fazio wrote home in 1954 that there were beacons in the sky over County Mayo like lavish, celestial messages, stars, fat, puffed out stars over a flat landscape which ran with stones and splintered rocks. From that letter on, Gisella wanted to join her brother in this country, Ireland, and in particular in the country within a country which the West of Ireland, Olivieri's stamping ground, seemed to comprise. In fact it was not just Gisella who followed her brother to Ireland but two other brothers. Olivieri had laid claim to a few shelled-shop premises on the main streets of decrepit towns and was turning them into cafés. Old counters swore with the pain of being renovated – drapery store counters, millinery counters – and being turned into food counters. Run-down streets, dowdy town halls baulked at these new spots of energy but there they were, the gleaming Di Fazio façades, usually a sanguine red which retained its freshness long after it was painted and reminded Gisella when she arrived of one of her reasons for leaving Italy, wanting to forget.

Olivieri Di Fazio, then a young man of twenty-five, with the curly, pale copper Di Fazio hair, had encountered Breda Finuacane on her pilgrimage to Assisi in the holy year, 1950, on one of those trips she took away from the focus of her pilgrimage. He encountered her in a village square and walked, almost mechanically, up to her, his smile somehow electrified by her strangeness, red, flossed hair, a face with all the dramatic brown twinges of a bog in it.

She would gurglingly relate that incident for years afterwards,

becoming, unnoticed to herself, plump and grey, in the telling
of it, though still retaining the floss in her hair, a Virgin Mary
pale-blue coat on her springy bosom in the café which she and
her husband looked after. Near the café was a bog, a bog coming
close to the main street, the bog a sea behind the main street, a
reminder with its few, isolated lights of the fatalities of life. It
was these lights which inspired Gisella to christen her café The
Tipperary Fanale, 'The Tipperary Beacon', though her café was
not situated in County Tipperary. It was as if she, like a dazed
traveller, had mistaken her location at first but in fact she just
liked the name Tipperary. It was in a song she remembered
from childhood and she was surprised to find that Tipperary, a
verbal signpost of her childhood, was to be found in Ireland.

Her husband had the cement business and the builders'
providers business behind the café. There was also a shed full of
wood chippings there, the chippings spilling out into the sun,
blond, and giving off an immaculate smell at odds with the
smells of the rest of the yard, and which was about her only
reminder of Italy in those first few years of marriage, the smell
of the wood chippings invoking the smell of the covert yet
spacious depths of forests near her home in Italy.

The Di Fazios had set up in Ireland very swiftly, thanks
initially to the benign lump of money left to his son-in-law by
Breda Finuacane's father who died after the marriage between
his daughter and the young Italian, without much delay.
Olivieri started a small industry and his brothers came and
fostered some of the cafés. Gisella opened her own, on the
premises of her husband's house. She'd met Ciarán Ward
shortly after arrival in Ireland and allowed herself to be wooed
by him, in the spirit of swift Di Fazio nuptials on Irish soil. He
had blond hair that was leaving his head, came from County
Galway and held a suppliant hat in his hand in front of the suit
he always donned to make the point that he was interested in
her.

Gisella became an Irish girl. Her parents came to none of the
weddings in Ireland. One by one the Di Fazios were renouncing
their family in Italy, that grandmother with the pigeon silver
hair and the bottom that stuck out like that of a pigeon, a

worried arch on her nose, the grandfather who forever sat, still in black, on a bench outside the family home, his eyes hopeless, almost unmoving since the war, the parents who'd rarely come out of the house since the war.

After two sons she nearly forgot Italy but ironically the sons had Italian names, Vincenzo and Salvatore, and there were those links to Italy, the name over her café, the names of her sons, the café now the meeting place of both town bard – a national school teacher in a chocolate-coloured suit who spoke Russian and who wrote poems on children's school exercise books – and town profligate, a big, burdensome man in a heavy coat who exposed himself on the main street after midnight, pulling back that coat to surprise some homeward-going, dance-loving virgins.

There was a river in the town and Gisella sat by it and a sunbathed in summer; she wrote letters beside it, back home. Italian was breaking down and Italian words careered with English words on the page. She wanted to forgive the family secret but now family was integrated into Ireland, and the idea of forgiveness became distant. Her parents no longer seemed to belong to her. There was the warm air, sensuality of her legs, lightwaves behind *duomos* of tree tops on the other side of the river. A boy came to her one day beside the river when there were teddyboys, he one of them, about to emigrate to England, recognizing her from the café, and brought her under a hawthorn tree recently relieved of its blossom and made love to her, the white chest of his over-big, funereal black swimming togs wearing a little floret of ash hair. Later she heard he'd been killed working on a rail line by a juncture of a myriad rail lines in Birmingham.

Before long Vincenzo was as old as that boy. Vincenzo played on the local hurling team, covered his own languid white chest in the blue and white local stripes, emerged as a hero from one or two games which decided mastery, was hoisted on local shoulders where he fitted easily. Vincenzo was a photograph in the local press. Ancestral looks had emerged in him, black hair which spilt over his face in a furnace, cheekbones that cracked in an orange, painted colour, sculpted, berry lips. 'The Italian'

34

Vincenzo was called. As if he was the only one of them worthy
of his race. The 'the' becoming a gruffer 'de' with time on the
lips of men who spent most of their summer days fishing for
pike. There were forebodings in that. Vincenzo had been
assimilated into the preconceptions of Irish machismo. This
sense of machismo had been well fostered when, after a short
course, he got a job as a television repair man in County
Donegal. He chose the job because it brought him far from home
and allowed him to veer around roads under drunkenly
undulating mountains in a landscape at times harsh, unrelent-
ing, tobacco-coloured and at times a piquant green as if he was
on the loose in the Wild West. There was a lot of anarchy about
County Donegal. Little wayside post offices which also sold
sweets, 1950s cigarette signs outside as if they were messages
pleading vulnerability, cigarette smoke static over yellowed
cigarettes since the 1950s, being constantly robbed by IRA men
and little old ladies being gagged and tied up, their pale blue
uniforms still on, beside cages which boasted rare breeds of
budgie. In the meantime, while Vincenzo was acquainting
himself with burly and bearded hordes in pubs in Letterkenny,
raucously singing with them into the small hours, Salvatore, a
frailer specimen, was attending the local boys' school, attaining
academic honours. There'd been little communication between
them as they grew up, five years between them, and now
communication and liaison of personalities were extinct. Salvatore was the one who talked of Italy, who reminded Gisella
when it was early spring near her home in Italy, who quested
for Italy with the determination of a catechetics student. He
wore his hair in an aggravated thickness as was fashionable in
the mid-1970s; a nonchalance about his shoulders in their
anaemic anorak. 'Salve' the local boys called him. He had his
great grandmother's nose, a bony and contorted arch to it. The
boys' secondary school was built in the 1930s, a bland, pale
square of a building. There were cherry blossoms outside, in
concentrated abundance where they were permitted, only at the
side of the building, and cherry blossom creeping around the
Ceylon Road like military marchers in a painting by Uccello
when Salvatore's father died suddenly in his late fifties. The

35

smallness of grief Gisella felt made her realize how little of a marriage there'd been, what a non-event of a relationship there'd been; all these years she'd been forgetting Italy behind the archetypes of another country – only the two sons the marriage produced seemed real, manifest, involving for her. So she withdrew from her husband's grave without grief and set back to work in the café which had now expanded into the adjoining premises and could cater for busloads of soccer players or busloads of pilgrims who'd set down in an interim between travelling on their bus to some site of a miracle or an apparition, the sight of these ladies under their scarves tucking into a meal of chips with pornographic deluges of ketchup on them becoming common. Gisella had walked away from her husband's grave but with a little withered pink chiffon scarf around her neck. It was taken as a nuance of Italy. But in fact it was an excuse to wear the brooch which clasped it, a brooch her youngest brother had given her years before, the one who was killed during the war.

'Madame,' the smelly, aged town profligate called her over, 'Madame, I sympathize with you.' He took her hand and manouevred it in his, feeling for her ring with the jade in it. The town poet said: 'Your heart will go down to the grave with him only to fly out. I know what it feels like.' His mother had died the year before. Vincenzo was home, having taken over the cement and builders' providers business, working away in the yard.

He was changed, squatter, masked in a fluffy and aggressive-looking beard. There was even a little touch of a Northern accent in his Southern accent, the Northern accent of County Donegal, a twin accent to that of the television world of Northern Ireland troubles, County Donegal she'd forgotten, hemming in the Northern Ireland state in fluid little crevices. These crevices were the ones IRA men on the run jumped over. Gisella thought, incongruously: 'He has an IRA accent.' There was a little pub in town which had the tricolour always unfurled on the wall and this was the pub Vincenzo went to now. There were dark congregations under this flag. But Vincenzo's demeanour insulated him from questions; he was very much the male presence; the fulcrum. He took over, swinging with his arms and working in the yard. He cut his beard off and cut his hair to marry. That was the first time Gisella's parents came to Ireland.

There was a photograph taken in the fair green, near the hotel, all the Italians and Irish, Gisella's parents and the young nephews and nieces from Italy, the brothers in Ireland, the sons and daughters of Gisella's brothers, but prettiest of all were three Italian nephews who'd come with Gisella's parents, three mascots, all of her part of Italy gathered into their faces, rounded, jovial faces with dumpy chins, dumpy eyes, freckles sieved on their faces, three identical suits on them, black shoes shining, blue, pink and blue again collars respectively open on them like the colours of shop fronts on a more flagrant Irish street.

After that there was collusion with Italy; letters; conviviality. Italy had made a mark in town and it was no coincidence that in St Matthias's Church on the hill, a squat Protestant building, during the autumn harvest thanksgiving the Italian Renaissance was mentioned by the rector as a metaphor of ever renewing hope. His daughters looked out from their pew, three girls with the hair of Botticelli angels. They'd had little affairs with Italian boys over for the wedding. They looked guilty now, their hair a pristine, almost silver blonde.

There was a rush of correspondence between Gisella and her mother; domestic things, ignored in and unfed into their minimal correspondence, were covered and quickly saturated. The rhythm of conversation started up in their correspondence, the frenetic, rising pitches of voices, the convulsed higher notes. The drama of conviviality, of closeness. It had not happened since before the war. Gisella's parents were old traitors. They were both emerging from their shame now for some crumbs of intimacy; old, mangy dogs both of them, lean in the stomach, dun coloured, their disproportionate heads drooping in front of them. Zammìo had died for them, had sacrificed his life for them or at least for Gisella's father when Gisella's father was abruptly going to be done away with, by hanging, by mutilation, by a gun, no one was sure. When a liberated, hysterical horde had gathered around the house where the black shirts had been burnt inside, one on top of another, the remains of them still in a grate, Zammìo had proffered himself; his chest had been very bold in that white shirt of his, it had stuck out, with adolescent defiance, the replete breasts of his chest. Maybe it was because he'd looked so well fed and defiant that the crowd took up his offer, ritualistically, and one of the men shot him in the head outside town. Afterwards the mob faded into non-existence and people of the village claimed they'd had no part in it; that this mob was comprised of inhabitants of the fields, the mountains, the borders of one distant field and another. Everybody had it mentally annihilated. There was a truce in that. Zammìo was buried and it might have been that he'd never lived. Gisella had taken the white shirt with the blood on it off his body and walked with it as though with a wounded bird whose life could still be saved. She'd walked as though hypnotized, in the direction of the village church. But there she'd found a flock of geese who'd escaped from the war and, suddenly screaming, she left the white shirt in the holy water font parched of water, three saints sculpted at the base of the font, three indifferent medieval male presences.

'Mrs Ward, I'm sorry to hear about Vincenzo. But it's still a good cause after all. He was doing it for Ireland.'

Two years after his marriage Vincenzo was taken away after a Garda swoop on The Tipperary Fanale and particularly on the yard at the back and convicted of manufacturing cement containers for bombs and arranging their transport up to the Donegal and Tyrone border. Nobody else in the family had known; nobody could have known. The ordinary-looking containers could have been anything in the way of industrial implements. Vincenzo and his wife had lived in the adjoining house to Gisella, on the expanded premises of The Tipperary Fanale. A flat had been made for them on the first floor. The wife, a girl from the outer townlands, now left the flat, arranged a legal separation – realizing she'd never really known Vincenzo very well – and the last that was heard of her was that she was a secretary in a modelling agency in Dublin, male modelling it was said, as well as female modelling.

The first time Gisella saw Vincenzo in prison – it was summer – he had a little nugget of black hair in the middle of his chest which despite summer was very white, his shirt off and she was reminded of Zammìo's chest. Nakedness was the demesne, the password of Irish politics. But Vincenzo's beard was shaved, he looked changed, his hair was neater. He was an adolescent among other adolescents and among hairy specimens of Irish heroes. The building was unwisely built. You might have been entering Auschwitz. It took you in a grey, Victorian grasp and seemed not willing to let you out. The summer heat had denuded the yellow irises growing in the town river, right down to their feet. They stood up, vacantly, from the water and little spirals of mud patches. 'Vincenzo.' The young man on the other side of the bars was a stranger, someone whose development she had ignored for years. When the image had become explicit, that of the Irish revolutionary, the politics went. Confronting her was just a pale, adolescent-looking shell.

Observing his neat, fashionable haircut she informed him that the barber, Gregory De Mare, at home had died, a man of reputed French Huguenot extraction, who'd clipped away in town with scissors since he'd gone bald at the age of twenty-two, only a black bushy tail left around his head since that time.

Vincenzo did not respond. She saw not just a prisoner behind bars but a prisoner of his own self-deceptions; only now that he was jailed was Vincenzo changing and a sensitivity, always implicit in him, not just emerging but enveloping him. The shaved, almost wounded-looking jaws were evidence of this. He looked at her with another history from that of Ireland, one she'd tried to repress. He looked for the first time as if he was acquainted with his origins, cut off from them for a long time, with only debased superficialities connecting him with them. 'De Italian.' A young man looked at her with a face that wanted to go back to where it rightly belonged but could not, among the pale florets of young men's faces standing around a dancefloor in her adolescence.

The people of the town were subdued, charitable in their

response to the event; she could take a bus back to the town as though to a bosom whose darkness would take hold of her and let her lose her splintered and throbbing heart in it.

It was not an unusual story in Ireland at the time; in fact it was in many ways unsensational; only 'The Tipperary Fanale' gained from it and sent out new, dangerous signals which allured many more people into it.

2

To everybody's surprise Salvatore, the frail, literary-shouldered one, decided to study engineering at Galway University. He wanted something as an antidote to the works of literature he read all through adolescence. He began to study in a rectangular modern building. He still moved around, in that fawn anorak. He started the year Vincenzo went to prison.

Two boys; Salvatore had always felt repressed by Vincenzo. Now that Vincenzo was in prison Salvatore began playing football in Galway, running around a muddy field near the lake, more for the colour of the soccer jerseys than anything else, bright red. He enjoyed pushing forward his legs as he wore the bright red jersey, exhibiting himself with drama. It was his invocation of Italy.

And as Salvatore was becoming more physical, even going for winter swims in the sea at Blackrock, exposing a gauche, white, though oddly full body with embarrassed spider-grey hairs on the legs, Vincenzo was conversely becoming literary in prison, poring over books on religious matters, inspired by an IRA colleague who decided to turn to God but not the God of the religious paintings in the church in Ballymurphy, Belfast but a more tender, less Irish God.

Near the prison lived a Protestant parson, once parson in the environs of Walsingham in Norfolk, England, and this man in his cottage with its honey-coloured thatch was making a study of the Gnostic gospels and their relation to the cult of Isis in Egypt. He had little pamphlets printed by a local press which purported to presage a new age of peace. These pamphlets had got into the prison and to the IRA man, Vincenzo's friend. An IRA warrior became docile, ameliorated by what he read, his face frankly shedding its beard and shining with a kind of dazed gladness.

The parson tried to visit his new converts but this man, all in black, with the wide-brimmed black hat of a Victorian priest in Ireland, was considered by the prison authorities as a possible subversive, having no family business with the prisoners, and after a period of him dangling, literally – his figure was long and lean – in the waiting room he was turned away. The incident had only added an extra grimace to Vincenzo's face when Salvatore came to see him the Easter after he'd started at university. Outside in a yard men traipsed around, repeating the same patterns of walking, Irish heroes, now grey motifs against a grey background. Inside Vincenzo asked him, through bars, for certain books. So in the next months Salvatore ferried books into Vincenzo, books about the Egyptian cult of Isis, about the Gnostic gospels, about the symmetry and mathematics of Chartres Cathedral. In a prison cell Vincenzo had started his own renaissance.

3

Easter 1984 there were prints of Botticelli paintings on the wall of The Tipperary Fanale, over the trough of bubbling chips, a rectangular tableau of economically muscular Italian soccer players in demon red. The place had changed; the time had changed; Vincenzo was being let out of jail a year later. Gisella, her hair having turned from copper to grey, was going back to Italy that Easter, for a wedding, her first time to Italy since she'd left. The grey of her hair was not the grey of wisdom, she'd lost two sons, one to jail, the other to England – Salvatore had given up his studies and was being very successful in the insurance business in London, making a lot of money, having already purchased a flat. He'd tired of academic things, ideas. He was gruff and well dressed now. Vincenzo, by contrast, was docile and, Gisella thought sometimes, almost senile. They both seemed somewhat deranged and outside her scope, beyond the limits of her sympathy, not because she didn't want to care but because they had made themselves dream-like, their gestures had wrought an emotional collapse in her towards them; she had no language to translate their gestures for herself. She felt herself virtually impotent towards them. Her two sons gone from her nearest concern, her mind was preoccupied elsewhere. It was as if thoughts were rising over the landscape of her life, like marchers approaching over a distant hilltop. There was The Tipperary Fanale always to keep her thoughts from her, to buffet her against them. But they kept approaching, a funeral march from long ago, the bringing of a body from the countryside. She had to reckon not just with Zammìo's death but with all the filaments of adolescence she'd left behind in Italy. *The Sandpiper* starring Elizabeth Taylor and Richard Burton was playing at the town hall cinema for the umpteenth time when she left for Italy, persuading her customers away for the umpteenth time the night before she left, to see Elizabeth Taylor in a shaggy painter's tunic going out to encounter the sandpipers of beaches near Monterey. So few people realized that Gisella was packing. Her face had been a kind of cinematic experience for her customers for years, the attraction of momentary, inscrutable images on it.

That Gisella was making a much wider journey was only evident to Marylin, her main assistant, the night before Gisella left, in a gesture which scared Marylin. As the café was closing, emptied, Gisella reached a fingernail to the Italian soccer players on the wall and scratched one of their faces, leaving a visible abrasion in the picture and a surprised look in an adolescent face.

The plane journey was to Pisa; Dublin had looked jubilant in sunshine, inviting her to stay. The drone of the plane went away inside her, a fearful, tense, drilling reverberation, an anticipation of the echoes of war which would inevitably reach her in Italy.

Zammìo had brought a dead rabbit home one day, holding the rabbit by its hindlegs. The rabbit had been tortured. Zammìo had confronted his father with it as though confronting him with an image of his beliefs but Zammìo's father had only seen in the blood and mutilation a kaleidoscopic equivalent to the bolder passages of Italian history.

Gisella and Zammìo had buried the rabbit, holding one another over the clay when it was settled again. Zammìo's chest had been generous and unrecoiling against her body. Zammìo's body had notified her of the male body; she picked out other young men from the dancefloor but their neat chests, their laundered and genteel embraces always sent her back to Zammìo. There had been something burlier about his body which had made her inquisitive. His chest had grown bigger in the course of their affair, the breasts of his chest more rotund. That no one knew of their affair was a mark of their mutual deviousness and of their exhilaration with one another which determined them to keep the secret. That she had been pregnant by her brother when he'd died had been a secret she'd kept all these years. She'd gone to Florence to have the baby but lost it. A mangled embryo had merged into an image she'd kept with her all these years, that of a little boy, as heir to the love between herself and Zammìo and as mental talisman. At Pisa airport there was a little boy in a blue and white striped T- shirt who looked at her as if she was the mother he was expecting from the plane and then he looked away. She had registered the untroubled waves of auburn of his hair though.

After staying the night with relatives a car brought her through the hills; the yellow blobs of mustard-seed hills. Towers pivoted on hills, modern water towers and medieval-domicile towers. They refreshed themselves at an open air café in the hills which was packed with tourists but tourists from other parts of Italy. It was Holy Thursday. Light ran amok over the windscreens of jammed, parked cars. Gisella breathed deeply before getting into the car again. In half an hour she would be home. She was a grey-haired woman in a demure, grey Irish suit, a snakeskin handbag in front of her, acrobatic wriggles of red in the patterns of the bag. She looked almost like one of those pilgrims that alighted in her café. All she needed was the little vinegar or perfume bottle of holy water beside her, holy water scooped in the course of the pilgrimage. The sun in her hair made it look white and somewhat mad though. There was a green in her eyes which had not been noticeable for years but the green was part of a middle-aged woman's face now and not that of a girl and the green looked fierce and demanding among the pallor of skin and hair. Gisella clutched the handbag awkwardly. She had lost the language of Italian self-confidence with items like handbags.

There was a *fiera* in the village the first days she stayed in it. Young men came out on to the steps leading to the square in the late afternoons, ties on them, many coloured shirts, spectacular shouldered jackets. Old men mingled with almost unnoticeable movements with the boys. Young and old looked eventually like actors coming on stage for the applause at the end of a drama. The difference between the old men's faces and the young men's faces was that the young men's faces looked more faraway, more enthralled. Maybe it was because it was near Easter but there was something devotional and silent in the stance of the young men. The women just went home with bread. The young men had infiltrated the *fiera* with the gestures of standing too, silent effigies around the bumpers, the sun prodding purple and emerald shirts. In the evening the mystically unchanging village towers and the gaudy turrets of the *fiera* merged, the big wheel going around and around and making you dizzy to the music of young girls' rhythmic squeals.

She had not found what she had been expecting, the werewolves of history, public and personal, waiting to grab her. The werewolves had gone. But instead she'd discovered that she'd been grabbed by another country's history and inexorably trapped in it. The arc of Irish history, that perennial, green landscape haunting rainbow had touched her life and trapped her much more than Italian history had ever done. In trying to get away she'd made a cage for herself of much tougher wires. She was bound now, by her life, by her children, to Ireland's tragedies and mistakes. Italy was an escape for her, a revelation, maybe even a renaissance. The biggest revelation being that ghosts don't stay around. The village had lost its ghosts. But there was one ghost or remonstrance of the past that had stayed and flourished, the image of a little boy.

You have children but they are not your real children. There were children long ago who are more real for you. The image of the little boy had stayed with Gisella all these years. For some reason he wore a blue and white striped T- shirt now. When she bumped into a boy on the steps of the church on Easter Sunday the child in her mind suddenly had that boy's bony nose and ethereal cheekbones. There are things in you that grow and grow – ideas, put together from the bits of experience that confront you in everyday life. They are the things that ultimately save you from insanity. They are also the things that give you a pivot to escape from, to start again.

On Easter Sunday night Gisella managed to free herself of her female company, company of assorted ages, and saunter off by herself, cardigan hanging from her shoulders, and grasp something of the *fiera* at night by herself. A young man laconically looked at her against a rouge background, a few sharpshooters lined up beside him, backs to the *fiera*, aiming at targets patterned against the rouge. His arms were folded in front of him and his stance, like that of so many young men in this country this mesmeric weekend, distilled silence and seemed to challenge you into similiar heights of silence and stillness. This time Gisella was, guardedly, still and silent, looking, her body and head poised sideways, towards the boy. There was a tiny retraction in the arms of the boy but the eyes became bigger, bolder, more black hued. There was curiosity, indolence, respect in them. He knew this was someone different. They became sloe-black, child's eyes, expansive, unbiddable, direct. There was now contact made between them which she could not back out of. So she continued to be still and told the boy, by telepathic messages, the story of her life. There was a furnace in his black eyes when the big wheel swept into them and an explosion of his white shirt when some wagon lit up in its descent near him or some stall's light went on and off, catching him momentarily in going on. Stalls were lighthouses, signalling. Gisella went on. Stalls tried to ravish her, lighting up with their wares of pink teddybears with prostrate, gangly legs. Gisella had lost the boy. She encountered a man's face between a pile-up of porcelain, idiot-faced, bonneted dolls. He looked at

45

her accusingly. There were doughy jowls beneath his keenly unshaven face. She was one of them, the *fascisti*. He had the face of a cabbalist. There was enmity in it, contempt. Gisella had to go away with his spittle on her face. The spittle reflected the wounds of three awkward red bulbs. She was back at a *fiera* long ago, once when she tried to step out of the house despite her parents' warning. There had been red blotches on her white dress that night and they'd become further encumbered, at the back, her arms folded precipitously in front, by dashes of a purple substance someone had thrown. Gisella had not noticed until she'd got home. But something had been achieved that night, an attempt at freedom, a stubborn attempt to integrate herself into the *fiera* and dissolve her past in it. She'd come home though from the attempt, like a bird with a sprained leg and inanimate wings. But there had been still movement in those wings, a movement she'd tested more and more and finally became joyous and somewhat potent with. One day she took off.

'The Tipperary Beacon' waited for her in Ireland. There was a loose hair of heather, fallen from a bunch of heather further along the shelf, under the tableau of the Italian soccer players the night she got home, the café closed. It was already actually the small hours of the morning. Her fingers pulled the hair of heather over and off the shelf where dust had been allowed to accumulate. It came as no surprise to anyone when a few months later she sold The Tipperary Fanale and returned to Italy, waiting first to bring a son who had an Irish tricolour inerasibly tatooed on the billow of slightly jaundiced muscle on the uppermost part of a feebler and more impotent arm.

The Airedale

The door of their house and the side gate to the archway leading to their yard, their proliferation of sheds and subsequently to their garden were painted fresh bright green. Green was the colour of the door and the side gate of the last house on the street, the house just before the convent. The nuns were always eager to get hold of the house and they did eventually. If you pay a visit to the town now it is merely an eventual part of the convent premises.

The stone of the house was dark grey and if you peeped through the bony windows you'd see shining wooden floors and above them paintings of the maroon and purple mountains of the West. We lived in the Western Midlands. East Galway. Mrs Bannerton was from Poland. She had blonde sleeked hair. She had taken a bus from the war and arrived in Ireland. In Dublin she'd married a surgeon. They lived now in our town. Denny was the son. Their one child. He was my friend.

I came from a family of five brothers. There were certain obscenities within my family. I can now see that friendship was one of them. Denny should have been from a suitable class background for closeness with me but my mother detected something she did not approve of there. Looking out the window at Denny trailing along on the other side of the street, beside rugged curtains she spat, 'You're not to play with him. He's wild.'

Denny was wild; he had wild chestnut hair, wild confluences of freckles, wild and expansive short trousers. He kept a milling household of pets, lily-white, quivering-nosed rabbits, garden-trekking tortoises, cats of many colours, at one stage a dying jackdaw, but monarch among the pets was Sir Lesley the Airedale. Denny tended his menagerie carefully, kneeling to comb the fur of cats and rabbits with a horn comb he assured me had been part of his grandmother's heirloom in Lublin. Later discovering that Lublin had been the site of a concentration camp struck home memories of a childhood where imaginary storks cascaded over a town which often looked, in its loop of the river, that it had been constructed as a concentration camp. Denny in white sleeveless jersey and white trousers combed a cat's fur and muttered a prayer he insisted was Polish. It was in fact gibberish. Denny did not know a word of Polish because his mother refused even to speak a consonant of it. Some languages are best forgotten. The town had its language. My family had its language. But the Bannertons spoke a different language and I owe them something; I owe them what I am now, for better or for worse. Denny's gibberish addressed to one of his cats is a language I still hear. We move from one country to another; we move from one language to another. But certain remembrances bind us with sanity. Denny's addresses to his cats is one of them for me. Another is the red in Denny's hair. Denny's red. My own hair was dull brown and I always vied for red hair so when I first came to live in this city I had a craze and dumped a bottle of henna into my crew cut, stared into my eyes in a mirror then and saw myself as an inmate in a concentration camp.

Denny and I sat together at school and we heard the words of William Allingham together:

Adieu to Ballyshannon! where I was born and bred
Wherever I go, I'll think of you, as sure as night and morn.

That we were elevated at an early age by the romance of words was also a saving grace of this town. The speaker of these words, a grey-haired headmaster with a worn and lathery black leather strap, is now lying in his grave. After doing his purgatory for the mutilation of poor boys' hands – boys from the 'Terrace', the slum area of town – he will surely be transported to heaven on a stanza of Thomas Moore. That was the duality we lived with. But Denny's home in the afternoons dominated at school. Toys on the wooden floor were trains winding through central Europe. Snow toppling on the trains – litter from Denny's hands. We saw a midget woman alight from a carriage on the floor, look around her and wander through the bustling streets of an anonymous central European city.

Mr Bannerton had a large penis. From Denny I first heard mention of the word 'penis'. He kept me in touch with his father's and mother's attributes. I presumed Mr Bannerton's large penis was to do with his medical profession.

Denny taught me history; the entire history of the world; he knew this from books; Denny read Dickens and Louisa M. Alcott. These authors owed their life in the town to Denny. He frequented their worlds. He borrowed their books from the library. Denny was a parent. At eleven he had a wide and middle-aged freckled face.

Everything was lovely about Denny, his father, his mother, his hair, his clothes, everything except his face. He had an ugly face. When I met him in later life he had kept that face like a chalking-up area for pain.

In Denny's home I first heard Mozart; I first spoke to a jackdaw; I first was kissed by a blonde woman; I first acquainted myself with the names of herbs. In Denny's home I first hated my mother and my father. I despised my brothers. There were no cats or no dogs in our home. No Airedales. I swapped passports in their home and took out citizenship of a country situated between bare wooden walls.

I was ten when Denny left. God threw snow out of a spiteful heaven. He was borne away in the furniture van. On the main street I cried. They were going to a city in the very South. I was wearing a short blue coat. Tears stung in my eyes and if I stay awake long enough at night I can still feel them.

All their property had gone, everything, except the Airedale. He'd been too big to carry away and whether they donated him to a neighbour or not he strode majestically around town for weeks. In the mornings on my way to school I nodded to him though he did not acknowledge me. Then one day I passed his carcass beside a dustbin. They left his carcass there for weeks, below the dustbin, until fleas got into it. I supposed it was to demonstrate to everyone the folly of being lofty and having once been the pet of a gifted family. The Bannertons went on to be part of a big city. There was an opera house in this city and a river which divided into two. There were many hills in this city and many churches. Now that I had been left my brothers turned upon me, beat me up, locked me into rooms on grey afternoons. It was a grey February afternoon for a long time now. One grey February afternoon I left to be a priest in Maynooth.

What happened in the meantime had been a kind of breakdown. My parents, fearful of consequences, confiscated stamp albums, books. Stamps were slightly suspicious, books were dangerous for me. They knew no better, my parents. They were peasant people, their parents having graduated to businesses in towns. The only book my mother had ever read was the penny catechism, and my father, a more jovial sort, had his joviality truncated by my mother. My brothers were all going to be accountants. At fifteen I borrowed by father's razor blade and slashed my wrists. Blood ran from the wound of a white hamster. They did not bring me to the main hospital but to the mental hospital. On the way there, like Denny, I began muttering gibberish. Gibberish saved my life.

Maynooth was rusted pipes alongside the grey walls of premises which were alleged to be haunted by catatonic ghosts; Maynooth was young clerics in black soutanes, hands digging deep into their soutanes, staring collectively at gutters; Maynooth was razor blades the colour of congealed blood, deftly taken from private lockers. There were sonorous prayers and professors of medieval philosophy who went around spraying snippets of Simon and Garfunkel. But eventually a prayer became too nasal for me; a part of my brain leapt into self-awareness again; before being ordained, a hitherto placid clerical student boarded a plane from Dublin to London, first having attended a film in his favourite cinema on Eden Quay. The city I arrived in was experiencing its first buffeting of punk hairdos; skies were bleached, dustbins overladen. Hands were generally shrouded in pockets. From a room in Plumstead I looked for work, got a job on a building site and a year later started attending a film school. Boats pushed past on the Thames outside my door. Plumstead marshes nearby conjured skeletal boats on the Thames. There was a ghost running through and through me as I sat, meditating, in my room in Plumstead. I could make little communication with fellow students. Something in me was impotent and my favourite occupation was sitting on a stool, meditating on my multiple impotences and creating a route out of them. One day I knew I'd walk out of inability. Charitable notes drifted through from Maynooth. There were short films made. There were eventually relationships made. Sex stirred like a ship on the Thames. But I touched one or two people. I made gestures to one or two people. I was released from the school with accolades. I made my first film outside school. A short film. On that ticket I returned to Ireland.

Adieu to Ballyshannon! where I was born and bred
Wherever I go, I'll think of you, as sure as night and morn.

A plane veered across lamb-like clouds. Below me was a Southern Irish city. My film was being shown in the annual film festival. I was sitting next to the window: I'd never been to this country before. I was an outsider now. I'd prepared myself and preened myself for that role. But a wind on the airport tarmac ruffled my demeanour and cowed me back again to Good Fridays and Pentecost Sundays on a grey small-town Irish street.

Cocktails were barraged towards the glitter of the light. Young women in scanty dresses and with silken bodies flashed venomous eyes at me. I was invited to bed chambers that always seemed by implication to be above the bars of cinemas. I declined these invitations. The night my film was shown, afterwards, I met Denny Bannerton. Dr Denny Bannerton. We said hello, made polite comments to one another, and arranged

to meet the next night. There was no award for my film. Silence.
Unmuttered blame. It had been a trip to Ireland though and I
was glad of it. In a gents' toilet full of mirrors I congratulated
myself on my black, polka-dotted tie, a narrow stripe of a tie
purchased on Portobello Road and subsequently endearingly
laundered and ironed. It was as if someone was affectionately
pulling my tie in the direction of London. But first I had an
appointment. A camera went off and took a photograph of me,
dark glasses on and a smile winter days living by London
cemeteries had given me.

A blank, broad freckled face with black glasses. A grey suit – a
collar and tie. Unusual accoutrement for a film reception.
Denny's face was still the same in a way. We met in a pub the
night after. The night was young Denny explained when we
met; there were many bars in this city to travel through. I sat on
a high stool and gazed into a purple spotlight falling on a many
ringed male finger. We had ventured into the gay scene of this
city. We were about to step further.

Swans, very clean swans; little neon-emblazoned retreats;
hills; wave-like lanes. A spiralling journey. Conversation. I was
the film maker. Denny Bannerton was an auspicious and regular
part of the newspapers and behaved as such. I was treated to
propaganda. I listened to the water, the breeze and the swans.
The tricolour flew for some reason over a Roman pillared
church. As Denny's conversation battled with the breeze, as
young men in white shirts behind counters, glasses being
cleaned in their hands, enthusiastically saluted him among
purple light, I made a mental film of his life.

The most important discovery in Denny Bannerton's life had
been that of his homosexuality. He discovered at thirteen. With
a white rabbit. In the back garden of a red suburban house. The
tenderness of his impediment connected him with inmates in a
concentration camp near Lublin. He was still in short trousers at
the time. Broad, blank-faced, at fifteen he had an actual beauty.
He had a brief affair with a corporeal monk who was directing a
Gilbert and Sullivan operetta. Afterwards, having been rejected
by the monk, Denny's face resigned itself to ugliness. At

university he took girls out. But such relationships quickly collapsed. As a young doctor he toured the world, had posts in Iran, in Venezuela, in Bristol. He returned to Ireland. Returning to his city in the south he announced his homosexuality. Affairs with Moslem, short-socked boys in the oil deserts. An affair with a piano-playing prodigy in Caracas. Nights of promiscuity in Bristol. Back home he politicized his loneliness. A doctor, he travelled the city with an expansive rose on his lapel. He was in the newspapers. He wrote irate letters to editors. He was a mirage on television discussion programmes. He'd peculiarly found his way home.

The questions asked of me were for the most part very factual; I knew what he was driving at. What were my sexual proclivities. I refused to answer. I just allowed myself to be led and occasionally I indulged in reminiscence. But it seemed reminiscence brought me back further than a garden. It brought me to a concentration camp on the suburbs of a Polish city.

Some of the nights in the desert had been like a concentration camp for Denny; the hot air, the arid flesh. Petrol had burned like pillars of flame. They had returned him to a geography before birth. Shirts were purple and pink in the dimly lit bars we slipped through. I was introduced to many people. A blond, furry-haired boy revolved his hand in mine in the pretence of shaking it. There had been the question of where Mrs Bannerton had really been from but now I knew. She'd been a mutual mother. Denny yapped on in a flaxen brogue, regardless of the images in my mind, furnaces lighting the night on the perimeter of a concentration camp in Poland.

Whether in reality or in dream she had traversed that camp. The skeletons had piled up in the dark. She'd heard the screams from those freshly dying. But in the middle of the skeletons and the screams she'd had an intuition of a limestone street, of an oak tree over a simple and pastoral pea garden, of an Airedale.

'So you're the film-maker. Heard your film was lousy. What are you doing beyond there in England? Pandering to Britannia. You should be home and drawing the turf of our native art.' An academic's lips seared with effeminacy. A gold chain sheathed the brushing of black hairs on display in the 'v' of his pastel-blue shirt, the chain sinking into a tan picked up in Mexico. 'You're one of the quislings who won't admit they're queer.' He was asking me to concede my ratio of queerness. I said nothing, looked to the photograph of a scarlet-sailed yacht in Kinsale. Denny muttered something about camera work. The one word reserved for special treatment by the academic was Britannia; I saw a spring shower dripping off a stone, slouching lion.

Back in the night Denny ran down the list of his endeavours to bring gay liberation to Ireland; planting flags on the top of low, buttercup-covered mountains, leading straddling tiny marches through the city, chaining himself to the pillars of the town hall. He'd been wearing a brown T-shirt the day he'd chained himself to the town hall. Not a grey suit as now. A breeze from the sea suddenly slapped me with a drop or two of rain on the face.

The edges of her hair had burned against the lights of the concentration camp; again and again she strode across my vision. She wanted to exorcise it. She'd come a long way. Suddenly she'd been in Ireland and she'd lain down.

'My ma discovered I was gay. She was informed by a neighbour I was gay. She wasn't sure what that meant but contacted the mother of a boy who was known to be gay. That woman declared "Mrs Finuacane don't fret. There were always gay men and women in Blarney but they didn't have the word for it then." '

I was speaking to a youth in one of the bars, interviewing him really. His hand was on a pint of Guinness. These rests in pubs interspersed with Denny's intense and self-engrossed mouthings.

In the same pub as I spoke to the boy I enquired about Denny's mother. She had stepped from a red brick suburban house into a big red brick hilltop mental hospital. Denny's mother had begun to eat her own fur coats. She was totally mad, Denny said. Totally mad.

In the Airedale I had seen it all; a crossroads. Denny had gone his way. I had gone mine. But some creatures lie down and die. Living becomes too much for them. Memory becomes too much for them. What she remembered I did not know. Could only guess. But she and her household of deranged hamsters had given me a residence in my mind. A new home. I had gone from their house, their world, with a life I would not otherwise have had; Denny had departed to this world. There'd been a juncture. An Airedale had marked the crossing. But a woman had held its thrall.

What had really caused an eddy in my gait had been the way Denny had referred to his mother. It was as if there was plain reason to be dismissory about her. She had sunk for him. Legend and myth had walked out of his life but I had cherished it. She had grown for me. She had marched across nights for me. In fact the first film I made at film school I had thought of her. The blonde, ice maiden-faced Polish lady. The lights had centred on her. When Denny had made his farewells I headed on into the night. There was a lot of way to go.

'See you now. Good luck with the films. I might see you tomorrow.' The phrases rang in my ears. I shovelled my hands into my jacket. Denny was an arabesque of remarks. But I had sauntered away from the Airedale a long time ago in this predestined black jacket. There were already films in my face and Denny had already changed in slinking away. There were worlds and corrosive thoughts to stride through tonight.

'Goodnight. See you.' There'd been a room in her mind. A chamber of torture. It had not necessarily been a concentration camp, the proximity to a concentration camp, but the experience and anguish of war. The worst anguish of surviving it. Storks and domed palaces had perished in this war. But she had survived.

The scintillating blonde-haired lady in the garden imperiously called to her husband. 'Bring me some lemonade.' A white rabbit stuck its ears up at her. I watched from behind an oak tree, my right hand clinging to the hoary bark.

The lights focused in on a girl's face. She had the features of Mrs Bannerton. Why do I remember this face? What had this face to say for me?

The city at night wound on. I unravelled the streets. There had been a point on which I had coincided with this lady. You go past pain. You come to meaning. I jotted little sentences in my mind. The city by the river, its slim outlying houses, was Italianate.

The first time I made love to a woman I thought of her. Her buttocks had asserted themselves through summer dresses, the disdaining quiver at the side of her buttocks. That quiver had said a lot. 'I'm not happy here. I'm not happy here.'

In the first few years after they went I used jumble words on blue squared paper at school; 'loss', 'severity'. Gulls had looked in on me, perching by an inedible crumb. I wanted to write to them, to all of them, but letters seemed inadequate to contain my feelings and anyway envelopes too frail to contain such corrosive letters as they might be. So I allowed myself to suffer. The Airedale had died. John F. Kennedy had died. My mother bought me a white sleeveless jersey one Christmas. At that point the Bannertons' house had been turned into classrooms by the nuns.

I'd wanted to write to her as well as to Denny. A letter to her had composed itself over my adolescence. There was place of pain we shared with one another. Not having any brothers I got on with I invented brothers in others, in boys who filtered through school – off to England after a short spate of studying at the priest-run boys' secondary school. There was chestnut hair, there were certain chest muscles behind white jerseys I envied in other boys. Boys from the 'Terrace'. Dionne Warwick sang me into a night of suicide. I woke up in Poland.

'Dear Mrs Bannerton . . .' Always there was a beginning of a letter to her. But after my exercise in suicide attempts whatever they did to me in the mental hospital part of my brain slumbered. They had cajoled me into their universe. Maynooth College, its black bricks, was a logical upshoot from that universe.

On a night vaguely ingrained with rain in a hilly city in the very south of Ireland I finally scrambled off that letter to Mrs Bannerton. She was in a mental hospital in the vicinity, a house I thought I detected, shining with a light or two on a hill.

The times I was on the verge of doing something truly disastrous – being ordained a priest – when there was the immediate imminence of some irreparable lunacy she stopped me. She took strides with me when I was in my black soutane. It was that room that carried me from Ireland to England. The room where her blond hair had looked red. Where toy trains spun around. Where trains stopped in towns you crept out into and had cold eggs showered in paprika in small cafés, the autumn sunshine shining through white wine and a leaf sweeper singing like a minstrel outside.

As a child I'd run up that street and peer in. There had been many ways of approaching a sight of the inside of that home. In the grey convent yard, a proudly decked member of the convent band, in claret dickie bow (which alternated occasionally with a miniature scarlet tie), white shirt, white long trousers, clashing a triangle, tripping in my clashing of it, one blue eye on the Bannertons' garden. What were Mrs Bannerton's limbs up to? Through the oblong window that stretched itself with narrowness on the street level you saw the brown wooden room and the journeys that the trains encompassed. Your mind gyrated with Europe's railways. Sometimes she stood in the middle of that room returning over these journeys, trembling in a leafy tight summer dress in the room. There was a person or a budgie she spoke to often. If it was a budgie it was to be seen, a cheeky lemon and lime thing. If a human being he was invisible. There were also ways you spied into that house in your dreams, through the chimney, on that roof that sent slates flying down in March. One night I travelled in the sky over their house on a broomstick and in my magician's capacity observed her dreams, trains snuggling into stations packed with marigolds and girls. But even being inside the house was always just an attempt. There were barriers. I was not one of them. The Airedale disdained me with one eye.

'How are you?'

A middle-aged man in a Charlie Chaplin-type bowler hat cascaded into me in the night. 'You're the young man who makes the films.' As a celebrity in my own right I sat beside him on a high stool in a late night café on a hill, Elvis Presley in maroon and pink on the wall, looking as if he'd been blasted on to it, as we discussed my films and my intentions with new films. As a *cappuccino* lever was pulled down – the café was Italian – a voice in my head in a County Galway accent said, 'Now you are their world.'

A woman in a room crossed her own barrier to be again in the boulevards and the parks of childhood. The edges of her hair had been red in remembrance. They had stood out, flames. Mrs Bannerton had had red hair as a child. She'd coveted a wooden sleigh with emerald tattoos on it. I too had a barrier to cross to remember. In the night my relatives webbed in me, no longer the demons I'd always presented to myself, but innocent. My mother, her frail sisters beside her, on station platforms in June during their youths. Many of my mother's sisters had died. Of purple lilac. Of tuberculosis. Purple lilac had flagged on russet, peeling railway bridges. Further back there was a room in history. A concentration camp. A war. A famine. There had been an operating theatre where innocence and joy had been removed. I had to make my way through ancestral minds to the joy in myself. The task in a black jacket seemed easy.

'Dear Mrs Bannerton . . .'

It was not to her I ended up giving most of my thoughts but to the young man I'd spent the evening with, her son. Whether we knew it or not those times we enacted pageants in the thick shrubbery outside the men's club – a black canvas-covered hut – we were seeking to return to a corner of history; Ireland before subjugation. In white bed sheets we had been the kings of an undefiled Munster and undefiled hobgoblin world. The garden had pointed the way to an innocence. That oak had shaded the wounds of history; the memory of war. It had covered a part of a human being quaking because the sores distributed on her body were not apparent.

'There was a bus; there was a journey. I'm not sure any more what I left behind. I just remember a little boy in white trousers holding the white handbag of a woman. He was holding it up for the world to see. As if to ask why he was holding it. Why wasn't it with its owner who was probably dead or mutilated.'

The film scripts were beginning again. I could not stop them. A woman's voice reached me from the twinkle of a mental hospital light.

In a church at dawn under a cinder-blackened Christ I prayed for her and for her son who had disappeared into his grey jacket, into his spectacles and into the manifold expostulations of his cause. I tried to restate a part of myself I'd tried to forget. Pain too, the crossed mangled legs were necessary. They were a connecting point with the dots of our ancestors on the atlas. The world inside me now was created from childhood; from the gruesome logic of art. An attempt at art. But attempts at art could only lead back. To a room. In an ornately lettered mirror in a bar the edges of my hair were ghostly henna.

'We try to build; we try to grow. But we always build backwards. May God help me both to forget and to remember.' There were swans on the river. Graffiti flung itself against a urinal. There were turkey feet of aeroplane tracks through the clear sky. A path led out of here now. I had a ticket to depart. To leave a place where Mrs Bannerton was incarcerated, where Denny Bannerton fought among the profusion of media attention, where a garden had been cemented over and an oak tree slashed down. The blood from the oak tree landed on the pavement of this city. I wanted to say over again. 'Thanks. Thanks for giving me birth.' But a chill had entered the air. It fingered the exposed headlines of newspapers. This was no country. It was no place. It no longer existed for me. All I was aware of were the aeroplane tracks in the sky. But there was a country in me now. There was a demesne. Sometime in the middle of the night I had gone back and picked up a child who'd been waiting on a street in Poland for a long time. There was a country where my child could be born or failing that where I could give birth to the latent little boy in myself. The terms of reference had changed; the language had changed. The chill in the air here no longer tortured me. The fate of the Airedale no longer bothered me. Soon Mrs Bannerton and Denny Bannerton would be forgotten. But walking back to the hotel I heard what I had not permitted myself to hear for many years.

The sound of Polish.

Players

For the week they were in town each year they changed the quality of life in the town; everybody submitted to them, shopkeepers, bankers, the keepers of the law. There was a certain light-headedness in puritans and moral flexibility in bigots. They were the players, the people who came to town, performers of the works of Shakespeare ever since the distant, Eamon De Valera mists of the 1930s.

The Mahaffy family gave their name to the players and Ultan Mahaffy commandeered the players. He looked much frailer than before in October 1958 when they came to town; one local woman, a businessman's wife in a perennial scarf, referred to him, in passing, in a conversation on the street as looking now 'like a sickly snowdrop'. Ultan Mahaffy should have been happy because 1958 was the first year his only son Cathal had played in the plays since he'd been assigned the roles of little princes, doomed to be smothered, when he was a child. Cathal had rebelled against the artistic aurora of his family and fled this emanation when he was seventeen to work as a mechanic in a factory in Birmingham. On his return you could see what a strange-looking lad he was: when he had been a child it had been suppressed in him, squashed down, but now he was an albino-like twenty-two-year-old, the whites of his eyes pink roses, the chicken bones of his pale chest often exposed by a loose shirt, his hair shooting up, a frenetic cowslip colour.

This mad-looking creature had been given the parts of Laertes in *Hamlet* and Hotspur in *Henry IV Part One* in 1958. The prodigal son had returned and conformed to the family notion of the inevitability of talent in all its members.

The week before they came the nuns had put on a show in the town hall; really a deaf and dumb show, schoolgirls in tights, berets on their heads, rifles by their sides – borrowed from the local army – standing immobile in front of a small cardboard prison that housed a cardinal (you could see the cardinal's meditative and lowered head through a window, a red bulb behind the cardinal's head).

There had been a bunting, made by a nun, of tiny hammer and sickle flags above the stage and this, more than anything, had excited gasps from the women in the audience and a round of applause. You weren't sure if it was the cardinal they were applauding for his endurance or the clever idea of the bunting. But with the coming of the Mahaffys there was one thing you could be sure of: that the bleeding church behind the Iron Curtain could be forgotten for a week. Only the Lenten missions united people in such common excitement. Immediately prior to the Lenten missions it was the excitement caused by the anticipation of so many sins due to be expunged. Immediately prior to a performance by the Mahaffys it was the excitement of knowing that you were going to be deliciously annihilated for a night by the duress of a play.

Mr and Mrs Mahaffy stayed by tradition in Miss Waldren's Hotel at the top of O'Higgins Street. This hotel boasted a back garden inspired by the gardens of the local ascendancy mansion, the garden full, for all its smallness, of walks and willow trees and little ponds drenched by willow trees.

This atmosphere was considered appropriate for the heads of the company but all other players stayed as usual with the two Miss Barretts in a more humble bed and breakfast house on Trophy Street. One of the Barrett sisters was about thirty, the other was near forty, the younger bright, exuberant, bristling with the thought of continual chores to be accomplished, the older usually seated, meditative, lank and arched of cheek.

The younger, Una, was small, pudgy, her head powdered with anthracite black and celestial vague hair. The older, Sheona, was, by contrast, tall, demure, red-haired, the fluff of her red hair gripping her ears and her neck like forceps. They'd been parentless for a long time, running a bed and breakfast house since their parents died when Una had just entered her teens. They kept the circus people and the theatre people: many disreputables came to the house, of salesmen only licentious-looking ones, of lorry drivers only those continually drunk. Their family origins had become a mystery for many in town; it was as if they'd had no parents and stepped out of another planet very alien to this town because their manners and their decorum were different.

Of the two, Sheona was the most faraway. It was as if she'd spent a time in another country and was continually thinking of it as she sat by the natty peat fires that Una had prepared. She was queenly, erect, but was now nearing, without the sign of a man, the explosive age of forty.

Much satisfaction was expressed with this year's perform-ances: Cathal Mahaffy, with his mad, upshooting blond hair, was particularly singled out; the redness in the whites of his eyes seemed to be the redness at the bottom of the sky in the evening after they'd gone, the sky over the fair green where the marquee had been. But Cathal hadn't really gone with the show. He came back again and again between performances of the plays elsewhere and it took some weeks before the people of town realized that he was having an affair with Sheona Barrett.

The realization came in a week of tender weather in November when he was seen again and again bringing Miss Barrett on the back of his motorbike on the backroads between wavering, stone-walled fields in the countryside outside town. The sky was very blue that week, the weather warm, and Miss Barrett, the near forty-year-old, often wore a summer dress under a cardigan and nothing other than the cardigan for warmth.

How did it happen? What had been going on among the crowd at the guesthouse? More and more women peeped through the curtains and saw the giant tableau on the sitting room wall of Kylemore Abbey, Connemara, the tableau painted on to the wall by a destitute painter from Liverpool once, this work done in lieu of payment of rent. The painter had a red scarf around his neck and women in the town muttered that you'd have to be careful of his piglet fingers, where they went. Now they knew where Cathal Mahaffy's fingers went. They knew only too well. Sheona Barrett had shed forty-year-old skin and become a young woman.

It was Christmas which riled the women most though, Sheona Barrett going up to Dublin to attend a dinner dance with Cathal Mahaffy, at which the lord mayor of Dublin was present. She'd walked to the station, not got a taxi, and some people had caught sight of her on that frosty morning, of the erectness of her bearing and the pink box she carried in one hand. What had been in that pink box? And she still stood straight. People now, mainly women, wanted to knock her off balance. It was fine as long as the theatre came only once a year but now that it had been detained people were disconcerted. Superintendent Scannell, who always dressed in the same withered-looking, yellow ochre civilian coat, was seen chasing his civilian hat along O'Higgins Street one morning. A soldier's trousers suddenly fell down as the soldiers stood to alert in the square outside the church one Sunday morning. A teacher in the boys' national school suddenly started uttering a pornographic poem in the middle of a mathematics lesson. This man was swiftly taken to the mental hospital. A celibate, he'd obviously been threatened by a nervous breakdown for years.

But some other people were not so fortunate to get such an easy way out. The theatre had stayed in town and upset people, to the very pegs of their being, those pegs which held their being to the ground just as the players' tent was held to the verdant ground of the fair green by pegs.

Sheona Barrett did not seem even aware that she was upsetting people. That's maybe what upset them the most, that austere bearing of hers. It was a scandal but because it was a scandal that came from the theatre the scandal was questioned. This was the stuff of theatre after all, that people sat comfortably looking at. Now that it had been let loose on the streets you had to ask yourself: was the theatre not an intoxicating thing, like whiskey at a dinner dance? Did it not block out realities? In a way they envied Sheona Barrett for having taken something from a night of Shakespeare in a fair green and made it part of her life. They all dabbled with the thought of ensnaring some permanence from the theatre and when they realized it was impossible they decided, *en masse*, to destroy Sheona Barrett's relationship so they could have the theatre back for what it had been, a yearly festive balloon in their lives.

A Texan millionaire had come to live in a mansion outside town in 1957, a mansion in which the caretaker, who'd been there since the rich owners had departed to take up residence in Kensington, London, had murdered his half-wit brother. The millionaire was a divorcee and the parish priest had blocked the entrance to the mansion with his car one morning and stopped the millionaire's tomato-coloured American car from coming out. The priest had got out of his car and approached the millionaire whose head was cautiously inside the car under a wide cowboy hat and informed him that divorcees were not welcome here. The millionaire departed forthwith, leaving his Irish roots.

The same trick was got up with Miss Barrett but with less success because the parish priest was ill and his stand-in, Father Lysaght, a plump, berry-faced man with his black hair perpetually oiled back, was addicted to sherry, saying mass and giving sermons when drunk on sherry, mouthing out the usual particularities of Catholicism but given new accent on sherry. He was dispatched to pull back Sheona Barrett from her affair, arriving already drunk, was given more drink and spent the night on a sofa with Cathal Mahaffy, discussing the achievements of Cathal's father.

Eventually the priest began talking Greek because he thought that was appropriate, quoting poetry about carnal subjects from his seminary days, digging his snout-like nose into the air as he recited, and then he wavered and snortled his way home. The final agreement had been that only the theatre mattered, nothing else did, and the church and its sacraments palled in comparison to a good theatrical performance. The priest got to the presbytery gates, jolting out a refrain from *The Mikado* remembered from his days at boys' boarding school, boys in merry dress and many in ladies' wigs lined up to daunt the 1930s with colour and the smell of grease paint.

The relationship of Cathal Mahaffy and Sheona Barrett had

been given a safe passage by the church. Sheona Barrett, by her association with theatre people, had been elevated to the status of an artistic person and as such was immune from the church's laws. You had to titillate people through the arts with a sense of sin so as to reaffirm all the church stood for. A thread united Sheona Barrett to the artistic establishment of the country now and she knew this, becoming so faraway looking she looked almost evanescent, as if she was part of the clouds and the fields.

Cathal Mahaffy invoked her to many parts of the country and she went swiftly. The townspeople knew now that the girls had been left money they'd never spent much of before. That was evident from the way Sheona Barrett could so readily draw on those funds to get herself around the country. There'd never been any need of that money very much before. Una Barrett groomed her sister, settling her hair. A taxi was often called to speed to some desolate town in the Midlands, past derelict mill houses and past weirs and houses which handed on an emblem for brandy on their fronts, to one another, like a torch.

In August 1959 Sheona Barrett attended the Galway races with Cathal Mahaffy. Her photograph was in the *Connaught Tribune*. She looked like a new bride. In late September they spent a few days together, again in Galway. They sauntered together by the peaceful blue of the sea, holding one another's hands. Most of the holiday-makers had gone and they had Salthill to themselves. The sea was blue it seemed, just for them. The blue rushed at their lovers' figures. There was a happiness for them in Galway that late September. Sheona's hair was a deeper red and often there was red on both her cheeks, 'like two flowerpots', one bitter woman remarked.

Cathal Mahaffy's body must have been lovely. He was so lithe and pale. In bed with her he must have been like a series of twigs that would seem almost about to break making love to this tall woman. He looked like a boy still. He had this intensity. And he challenged you with his pale appearance, his albino hair, his direct smile. You always ended up for some reason looking to his crotch as his shoulders sloped in his act of looking at you directly.

It was also clear that Cathal's parents approved of the relationship or at least didn't object to it. They were broad-minded people. They were glad to have their son with them and he could have been making love to a male pigmy for all they cared it seemed. They had seen many sexual preferences in their time and a lifetime in theatre qualified them to look beyond the land of sex, to see things that transcended sex; comradeship, love, devotion to art. Art had guided their lives and because of this they themselves transcended the land of Ireland and saw beyond it, to the centuries it sometimes seemed from the look on Mrs Mahaffy's face as she stood on a green in a village, the light from a gap in the tent falling on her face. But there was always some tragedy at the end of the route of tolerance in this country.

Shortly before the players arrived in Sheona's town in 1959 Sheona was set upon in a routine walk by the railway station, near a bridge over a weir, and raped. No one could say who raped her but it was known that it had been a gang. She had been physically brutalized apart from being raped and mentally damaged. When she was brought to hospital it was clear that some damage was irrevocable in her. There was a trail of stains like those of tea leaves all across her face when she sat up in bed and her eyes stared ahead, not seeing what she'd seen before. Una Barrett was there, holding a brown scapular she'd taken from its covert place around her neck.

The performances were cancelled that year. There was a mysterious silence around the players. The probable reason was that Cathal Mahaffy had opted out of the main parts in two Jacobean plays that weren't Shakespeare's. He'd made off on that motorbike of his after seeing Sheona in hospital, to mourn.

A rape, a job of teaching someone a lesson, had gone wrong. There had been an excess of brutality. The youths who'd run away from Sheona through the thickets by the river had probably been put up to it by nameless and sinister elders in town. That was the hazy verdict handed down. There'd been many accomplices and people, in a Ku Klux Klan way, kept silent about the event, kept their lips sealed as if it had been a figment of someone's imagination and there were often irritated howls years later when the event was referred to.

66

Sheona Barrett ended up in a home in Galway and she is still there; someone who saw her says her hair is still as red as it was then.

Cathal left the players permanently after the tragedy of October 1959 which months later still spread disbelief. He continued in the theatre in a ragged kind of way for a few years, his most celebrated role being as a black, scintillating cat in one of Dublin's main theatres at Christmas 1960 but after that his appearances became fewer and fewer, until eventually he was down to secondary roles in discontented American plays in the backstreet and basement theatres of the city of Dublin.

But his good looks flourished, that appearance of his became seraphim-like, and he was taken up by a rich American woman who'd moved into a top floor flat in Baggot Street, Dublin, and he lived with her as her lover for a few years in this bohemian spell of hers, seen a lot with her in Gajs' Restaurant over its tables regulated by small bunches of red carnations or in narrow pubs packed with Americans and Swedes craning to hear uilleann pipes played by hairy North-side Dubliners in desultory red check shirts. He nearly always had a black leather jacket on as if he was ready to depart and move on and it was true that no relationship could really last in his life so haunted and fragmented was he by what had happened to Sheona Barrett; he felt irrefutably part of what had happened.

One day he did leave the American woman but she was already thinking of leaving Dublin so there was some confusion about his leaving her; no observer was sure which of the pair it was who sundered the relationship.

He spent a few months on people's floors, often on quite expensive antique carpets, around the Baggot Street, Fitzwilliam Square, Pembroke Road area of Dublin. The antique carpets were no coincidence in his life because he was actually working for an antique dealer now who had a shop on Upper Baggot Street and in Dun Laoghaire. The job was kind of a gift, kind of decoration for an aimless person and one Saturday when he wasn't working he did what he'd wanted to do for a long time, drive west on his motorbike to Sheona Barrett's town to try to find the answer to a question which had beleaguered his mind for so long; why, why the evil, why the attack, what had been the motivation for this freak outrage, what had been the forces gathered behind it?

But in the town he discovered that there were other explanations for Sheona's state as if she'd been ill all the time. Una Barrett was a housewife, a guesthouse keeper, a mother, the wife of a man who had Guinness spilt all over his already brown jacket and waistcoat. The day was very blue: in the square there was an abundance of geraniums being sold; the sky seemed specially blue for his visit. All was happiness and change here. The past didn't exist. He was an exile, by way of lack of explanations, from the present.

But the more he stuck about, wandering among the market produce, the farmers made uncomfortable by the fact he wasn't purchasing anything, the more he knew. People did not like happiness. They distrusted happiness of the flesh more than anything. The coming together of bodies in happiness was an outrage against the sensibilities. It not only should not be allowed to exist but it had to be murdered if it wasn't going to unhinge them further. A swift killing could be covered up, it could be covered up forever; only the haunted imagination would keep it alive and that imagination would, by its nature, be driven out of society, so all could feel safe. There was no home for people like Cathal Mahaffy who knew and remembered.

With money he got from an unannounced source he purchased a house in a remote part of County Donegal in the late 1960s; the house up on a hill overlooking the swing of a narrow bay. There was much work to be done on it, a skeleton of a grey house peculiar and abandoned among the boulders that all the time seemed about to tumble into the sea.

On the back of his motorbike he ferried building materials from Donegal Town. These were the hippie days of the late 1960s and blue skies over the bay seemed arranged to greet visitors from Dublin. Often people got a bus to Donegal Town and then there was a liberated jaunt on the back of a motorbike around twists by the sea. There were benevolent fields to one side, the green early Irish monks would talk about, and stone walls dancing around the fields, finicky patterned stone walls.

These fields stretching to one side of him like a director's hand Cathal was killed on his motorbike one June day, a Lawrence of Arabia in County Donegal, all his motorbike gear on at the time, helmet, black leather jacket and old-fashioned goggles – a caprice? You felt he was being relieved of some agony he could no longer bear, that the day in June was the last he could have lived anyway, what with the pain in him people had noticed, a pain that scratched out phrases by the half-door of his house, into the Donegal air outside when he was under the influence of fashionable drugs transported from Dublin.

One of these last phrases, these last annotations had been – a woman about to play in a 1930s' comedy revival in Dublin had sworn it, her lips already red for the part – 'I don't know why they did it. Why? Why? Why? The innocent. The innocent.' This was mistaken as a premature eulogy for himself and because of it all the young rich degenerates in Dublin who saw themselves as being innocent and maliciously tortured by society gathered by his grave in County Wicklow for the funeral, making it a fashionable Dublin event, a young man later said to have epitomized the event, a young man who wasn't wearing a shirt and was advertising his pale, Pre-Raphaelite chest in the hot weather, a safe distance up from the grave, his chest gleaming, under a swipe of a motorcyclist's red scarf, with sweat and with a hedonist's poise.

Among the crowd from Dublin there were some strange rural mourners but no one identified them and anyway they were jostled and passed over in the crowd so awkward was their appearance, so nondescript was their floral contribution. But someone did, out of some quirky interest, get the name of the town they were going back to out of them. It was Sheona's town and the name was said almost indistinguishably so heavy and untutored was the accent.

Ultan Mahaffy did go back to the town a few times after 1959. The company was smaller but the spirit was still high despite losses of one kind or another. The players were greeted in the town with solicitude rather than with reverence. They were tatty compared to what they had been and the marquee in the fair green came to look almost leprous, unapproachable.

In October 1963 Ultan Mahaffy had a strange experience in the town, one which made him shudder, as if death had sat beside him. A man approached him in Miss Waldren's hotel, a tall man under a yellow ochre hat, in a weedy, voluminous, almost gold coat – the colour of the coat evoked stretches in the middle of bogs, slits of beach in faraway County Mayo; it was a kaleidoscopic bunch of national associations the coat brought, but its smell was very definitely of decay, of moroseness.

'I beg your pardon, Mr Mahaffy,' a voice said. 'We respect you. You brought art to the town. You'll go down in history. You can't say anything to history. You can't say anything to history.' With that he turned his back and went off. What had he been saying? That Mr Mahaffy could not be impugned because he was part of history. Part of the history books like Patrick Pearse and Cúchulainn. But there had been others who were not quite so fortunate. Mr Mahaffy looked after the man and knew that he would not be coming back to this town again.

The following summer, before the new season, Mr Mahaffy had a heart attack in Blackrock Baths in Dublin while walking on the wall which separated the open air pool from the grey Irish Sea. He'd looked an exultant figure in his bathing togs before the heart attack, standing up there, stretching his body for all the children to see.

But anyway Mr Mahaffy's life's work had become irrelevant in Sheona Barrett's town. A few years before, on a New Year's Eve, when snow was falling, screens lit up all over the town with their own snow to mark the first transmission by Irish television.

Martyrs

Ella was an Italian woman whose one son had been maimed in a fight and was now permanently in a wheelchair, still sporting the char-black leather jacket he'd had on the night he'd been set upon. Ella's cream waitress outfit seemed to tremble with vindication when she spoke of her son's assailants. 'I'll get them. I'll get them. I'll shoot them through the brains.' The chrome white walls listened. Chris's thoughts were set back that summer to Sister Honor.

The lake threw up an enduring desultory cloud that summer – it was particularly unbudging on Indiana Avenue – and Chris sidled quickly by the high-rise buildings which had attacked Mrs Pajalich's son. Sister Honor would have reproached Ella with admonitions of forgiveness but Chris saw – all too clearly – as she had in Sister Honor's lucid Kerry coast-blue eyes the afternoon she informed her she was reneging on convent school for State high school that Sister Honor would never forgive her, the fêted pupil, for reneging on a Catholic education for the streams of state apostasy and capitalistic indifference. Chris had had to leave a Catholic environment before it plunged her into a lifetime of introspection. She, who was already in her strawberry, black check shirt, orientated to a delicate and literary kind of introspection. Sister Honor's last words to her, from behind that familiar desk, had been 'Your vocation in life is to be a martyr.'

The summer before university Chris worked hard – as a waitress – in a cream coat alongside Mrs Pajalich. Beyond the grey gravestone citadels of the city were the gold and ochre cornfields. At the end of summer Chris would head through

71

them – in a Greyhound bus – for the university city. But first she had to affirm to herself 'I have escaped Sister Honor and her many mandates.'

Ella Pajalich would sometimes nudge her, requesting a bit of Christian theology, but inevitably reject it. Ella had learnt that Chris could come out with lines of Christian assuagement. However, the catastrophe had been too great. But that did not stop Ella, over a jam pie, red slithering along the meringue edges, from pressing Chris for an eloquent line of heaven-respecting philosophy.

Rubbing a dun plate that was supposed to be white Chris wondered if heaven or any kind of Elysium could ever touch Ella's life; sure there were the cherry blossoms by the lake in a spring under which she pushed her son. But the idea of a miracle, of a renaissance, no. Mrs Pajalich was determined to stick the café bread knife through someone. If only the police officer who allowed his poodle to excrete outside her street-level apartment. Ella had picked up the sense of a father of stature from Chris and that arranged her attitude towards Chris; Chris had a bit of the Catholic aristocrat about her, her father an Irish-American building contractor who held his ground in windy weather outside St Grellan's on Sunday mornings, his granite suit flapping, a scarlet breast pocket handkerchief leaping up like a fish, his black shoes scintillating with his youngest son's efforts on them and his boulder-like fingers going for another voluminous cigar. 'Chris you have the face of fortune. You'll meet a nice man. You'll be another Grace Kelly. End up in a palace.' Chris saw Grace Kelly's face, the tight bun over it, the lipstick like an even scimitar. She saw the casinos. Yes she would end up living beside casinos in some mad, decadent country, but not Monaco, more likely some vestige of Central or South America.

'Chris will you come and visit me at Hallowe'en?' The dreaming Chris's face was disturbed. 'Yes, yes, I will.'

Summer was over without any great reckoning when Sister Honor and Chris slid south, through the corn, to a city which rose over the corn, its small roofs, its terracotta museums by the clouded river, its white Capitol buildings, a centrepiece, like a Renaissance city.

Sister Honor had imbibed Chris from the beginning as she would a piece of revealing literature; Chris had been established in class as a reference point for questions about literary complexities. Sister Honor would raise her hand and usher Chris's attention as if she was a traffic warden stopping the traffic. 'Chris, what did Spenser mean by this?' Honor should have known. She'd done much work in a university in Virginia on the poet Edmund Spenser; her passion for Spenser had brought her to County Cork. She'd done a course in Anglo-Irish literature for a term in Cork university. Red Irish buses had brought her into a countryside, rich and thick now, rich and thick in the Middle Ages, but one incandesced by the British around Spenser's time. The British had come to wonder and then destroy. Honor had come here as a child of five with her father, had nearly forgotten, but could not forget the moment when her father, holding her hand, cigar smoke blowing into a jackdaw's mouth, had wondered aloud how they had survived, how his ancestry had been chosen to escape, to take flight, to settle in a town in the Midwest and go on to creating dove-coloured twentieth-century skyscrapers.

Perhaps it had been the closeness of their backgrounds which had brought Chris and Honor together – their fathers had straddled on the same pavement outside St Grellan's Catholic church, they'd blasted the aged and lingering Father Duane with smoke from the same brand of cigars. But it had been their ever-probing interest in literature which had bound them more strongly than the aesthetic of their backgrounds – though it might have been the aesthetic of their backgrounds which drove them to words. 'Vocabularies were rich and flowing in our backgrounds,' Sister Honor had said. 'Rich and flowing.' And what did not flow in Sister Honor she made up for in words.

Many-shaped bottoms followed one another in shorts over the verdure around the white Capitol building. The atmosphere was one of heightened relaxation; smiles were 1950s-type smiles on girls in shorts. Chris found a place for herself in George's bar. She counted the lights in the constellation of lights in the jukebox and put on a song for Sister Honor. Buddy Holly. 'You go your way and I'll go mine.' A long-distance truck driver touched her from behind and she realized it was two in the morning.

She had imagined Sister Honor's childhood so closely that sometimes it seemed that Sister Honor's childhood had been her childhood and in the first few weeks at the university – the verdure, the sunlight on white shorts and white Capitol building, the fall, many-coloured evening rays of sun evoking a primal gust in her – it was of Sister Honor's childhood she thought and not her own. The suburban house, hoary in colour like rotten bark, the Maryland farm she visited in summer – the swing, the stars and stripes on the verdant slope, the first or second edition Nathaniel Hawthorne books open, revealing mustard, fluttering pages like an evangelical announcement. In the suburbs of this small city Chris saw a little girl in a blue crinoline frock, mushrooming outwards, running towards the expectant arms of a father. Red apples bounced on this image.

Why had she been thinking of Sister Honor so much in the last few months? Why had Sister Honor been entering her mind with such ease and with such unquestioning familiarity? What was the sudden cause of this tide in favour of the psyche of a person you had tried to dispose of two years beforehand? One afternoon on Larissa Street Chris decided it was time to put up barriers against Sister Honor. But a woman, no longer in a nun's veil, blonde-haired, hair the colour of dried honey, still tried to get in.

Chris was studying English literature in the university – in a purple-red, many-corridored building – and the inspection of works of eighteenth- and nineteenth-century literature again leisurely evoked the emotion of the roots of her interest in literature, her inclination to literature, and the way Sister Honor had seized on that interest and so thoughts of Sister Honor – in the context of her study of literature – began circulating again. Sister Honor, in her mind, had one of the acerbic faces of the Celtic saints on the front of St Grellan's, a question beginning on her lips, and her face lean, like a greyhound's, stopped in the act of barking.

'Hi, I'm Nick.'

'I'm Chris.'

A former chaperone of nuclear missiles on a naval ship, now studying Pascal, his broad shoulders cowering into a black leather jacket, accompanied Chris to George's bar one Saturday night. They collected others on the way, a girl just back from an all-Buddhist city in California, a young visiting homosexual lecturer from Cambridge, England, a girl from the People's Republic of China who said she'd been the first person from her country to do a thesis at Harvard – hers was on nineteenth-century feminist writers. George's bar enveloped the small group, its low red, funeral-parlour light – the lights in the window illuminating the bar name were both blue and red.

Autumn was optimistic and continuous, lots of sunshine; girls basked in shorts as though for summer; the physique of certain girls became sturdier and more ruddy and brown and sleek with sun. Chris found a tree to sit under and meditate on her background, Irish Catholic, its sins against her – big black aggressive limousines outside St Grellan's on Sunday mornings unsteadying her childhood devotions, the time they dressed her in emerald velvet, cut in triangles, and made her play a leprechaun, the time an Irish priest showed her his penis under his black soutane and she'd wondered if this was an initiation into a part of Catholicism – and her deliverance from it now. The autumn sun cupped the Victorian villas in this town in its hand, the wine-red, the blue, the dun villas, their gold coins of autumn petals.

Chris was reminded sometimes by baseball boys of her acne – boys eddying along the street on Saturday afternoons, in from the country for a baseball match – college boys generally gave her only one to two glances, the second glance always a curious one as she had her head down and did not seem interested in them. But here she was walking away from her family and sometimes even, on special occasions, she looked straight into someone's eyes.

What would Sister Honor have thought of her now? O God what on earth was she thinking of Sister Honor for? That woman haunts me. Chris walked on, across the verdure, under the Capitol building beside which cowboys once tied their horses.

The Saturday-night George's bar group was deserted – Nick stood on Desmoines Street and cowered further into his black leather jacket, muttering in his incomprehensible Marlon Brando fashion of the duplicity of the American government and armed forces – Chris had fallen for a dance student who raised his right leg in leotards like a self-admiring pony in the dance studio. The plan to seduce him failed. The attempted seduction took place on a mattress on the floor of his room in an elephantine apartment block which housed a line of washing machines on the ground floor which insisted on shaking in unison in a lighted area late into the night, stopping sometimes as if to gauge the progress of Chris's and her friend's love-making. In the early stages of these efforts the boy remembered he was a homosexual and Chris remembered she was a virgin. They both turned from one another's bodies and looked at the ceiling. The boy said the roaches on the ceiling were cute. Chris made off about three in the morning in a drab anorak, blaming Catholicism and Sister Honor, the autumn river with its mild, off-shooting breeze leading her home. Yes, she was a sexual failure. Years at convent school had ensured a barrier between flowing sensuality and herself. Always the hesitation. The mortification. Dialogue. 'Do you believe we qualify, in Martin Buber's terms, for an I – thou relationship, our bodies I mean.' 'For fuck's sake, my prick has gone jellified.'

Chris knew there was a hunch on her shoulders as she hurried home; at one stage, on a bend of the river near the road, late, home-going baseball fans pulled down the window of a car to holler lewdnesses at her. She'd never been able to make love – 'Our bodies have destinies in love,' Sister Honor rhetorically informed the class one day – and Chris had been saving her pennies for this destiny. But tonight she cursed Sister Honor, cursed her Catholicism, her Catholic-coated sense of literature and most of anything Sister Honor's virginity which seemed to have given rise to her cruelty. 'Chris, the acne on your face has intensified over Easter. It is like an ancient map of Ireland after a smattering of napalm.' 'Chris, your legs seem to dangle, not hold you.' 'Chris, walk straight, carry yourself straight. Bear in mind your great talent and your great intelligence. Be proud of it. Know yourself Chris Gormley.' Chris knew herself tonight as a bombed, withered, defeated thing. But these Catholic-withered limbs still held out hope for sweetening by another person.

Yes, that was why she'd left convent school – because she perceived the sham in Sister Honor, that Sister Honor had really been fighting her own virginity and in a losing battle galled other people and clawed at other people's emotions. Chris had left to keep her much-attacked identity intact. But on leaving she'd abandoned Sister Honor to a class where she could not talk literature to another pupil.

Should I go back there sometime? Maybe? Find out what Honor is teaching. Who she is directing her emotions to. If anybody. See if she has a new love. Jealousy told Chris she had not. There could never have been a pair in that class to examine the Ecclesiastes like Honor and herself – 'A time of war, and a time of peace.' Chris had a dream one night in which she saw Honor in a valley of vines, a biblical valley, and another night a dream in which they were both walking through Spenser's Cork, before destruction, by birches and alders, hand in hand, at home and at peace with Gaelic identity and Gaelic innocence or maybe, in another interpretation of the dream, with childhood bliss. Then Sister Honor faded – the nightmare and the mellifluous dream of her – the argument was over. Chris settled back, drank, had fun, prepared for autumn parties.

The Saturday-night George's bar group was resurrected – they dithered behind one another at the entrance to parties, one less sure than the other. Chablis was handed to them, poured out of cardboard boxes with taps. A woman in black, a shoal of black balloons over her head, their leash of twine in her hand, sat under a tree in the garden at a party one night. She was talking loudly about an Egyptian professor who had deserted her. A girl approached Chris and said she'd been to the same convent as Chris had been. Before the conversation could be pursued the room erupted into dancing – the girl was lost to the growing harvest moon. Chris walked into the garden and comforted the lady in black.

77

'Dear Sister Honor.' The encounter prompted Chris to begin a letter to Honor one evening. Outside, the San Francisco bus made its way up North Dubuque Street – San Francisco illuminated on the front – just about overtaking a fat negro lady shuffling by Victorian villas with their promise of flowers in avenues that dived off North Dubuque Street, heaving her unwieldly laundry. But the image of Sister Honor had faded too far and the letter was crumpled. But for some reason Chris saw Honor that night, a ghost in a veil behind a desk, telling a class of girls that Edmund Spenser would be important to their lives.

Juanito was a Venezuelan boy in a plum-red T-shirt, charcoal hair falling over an almost Indian face which was possessed of lustrous eyes and lips that seemed about to moult. He shared his secret with her at a party. He was possessed by demons. They emerged from him at night and fluttered about the white ceiling of Potomac apartments. At one party a young man, José from Puerto Rico, came naked, crossed his hairy legs in a debonair fashion and sipped vodka. So demented was he in the United States without a girlfriend that he forgot to put on clothes. Juanito from Venezuela recurred again and again. The demons were getting worse. They seemed to thrive on the season of Hallowe'en. There was a volcanic rush of them out of him now at night against the ceiling. But he still managed to play an Ella Fitzgerald number 'Let's Fall in Love' on a piano at a party. José from Puerto Rico found an American girlfriend for one night but she would not allow him to come inside her because she was afraid of disease, she told him, from his part of the world.

Chris held a party at her apartment just before the mid-term break. Juanito came and José. She'd been busy preparing for days. In a supermarket two days previously she'd noticed as she'd carried a paper sack of groceries at the bottom left-hand corner of the college newspaper, a report about the killing of some American nuns in a Central American country. The overwhelming feature on the page, however, had been a blown-up photograph of a bird who'd just arrived in town to nest for the winter. Anyway the sack of groceries had kept Chris from viewing the newspaper properly. The day had been very fine and Chris, crossing the green of the campus, had encountered the bird who'd come to town to nest for the winter, or a similar bird. There was goulash for forty people at Chris's party – more soup than stew – and lots of pumpkin pie, apple pie and special little coffee buns, specked by chocolate, which Chris had learned to make from her grandmother. The party was just underway when five blond college boys in white T-shirts entered bearing candles in carved pumpkin shells, flame coming through eyes and fierce little teeth. There were Japanese girls at Chris's party and a middle-aged man frequently tortured in Uruguay but who planned to return to that country after this term at the college. He was small, in a white T-shirt, and he smiled a lot. He could not speak English too well but he kept pointing at the college boys and saying 'nice'. At the end of the party Chris made love in the bath not to one of those boys who'd made their entrance bearing candles in pumpkin shells but to a friend of theirs who'd arrived later.

In the morning she was faced by many bottles and later, a few hours later, a ribboning journey through flat, often unpeopled land. The Greyhound bus was like her home. She sat back, chewed gum, and watched the array of worn humanity on the bus. One of the last highlights of the party had been José emptying a bottle of red wine down the mouth of the little man from Uruguay.

When she arrived at the Greyhound bus station in her city she understood that there was something different about the bus station. Fewer drunks around. No one was playing the jukebox in the café. Chris wandered into the street. Crowds had gathered on the pavement. The dusk was issuing a brittle, blue spray of rain. Chris recognized a negro lady who usually frequented the bus station. The woman looked at Chris. People were waiting for a funeral. Lights from high-rise blocks blossomed. The negro woman was about to say something to Chris but refrained. Chris strolled down the street, wanting to ignore this anticipated funeral. But a little boy in a football T-shirt told her 'The nuns are dead.' On the front page of a local newspaper, the newspaper vendor forgetting to take the money from her, holding the newspaper from her Chris saw the news.

79

Five nuns from this city had been killed in a Central American country. Four were being buried today. One was Honor.

When Chris Gormley had left the school Sister Honor suddenly realized now that her favourite and most emotionally involving pupil – with what Sister Honor had taken to be her relaxed and high sense of destiny – had gone, that all her life she had not been confronting something in herself and that she often put something in front of her, prize pupils, to hide the essential fact of self-evasion. She knew as a child she'd had a destiny and so some months after Chris had gone Honor flew – literally in one sense but Honor saw herself as a white migrating bird – to Central America with some nuns from her convent. The position of a teaching nun in a Central American convent belonging to their order had become vacant suddenly when a nun began having catatonic nightmares before going, heaving in her frail bed. With other sisters she changed from black to white and was seen off with red carnations. The local newspaper had photographed them. But the photograph appeared in a newspaper in Detroit. A plane landed in an airport by the ocean, miles from a city which was known to be at war but revealed itself to them in champagne and palm trees. A priest at the American Embassy gave them champagne and they were photographed again. There was a rainbow over the city that night. Already in that photograph when it was developed Honor looked younger. Blonde hair reached down from under her white veil, those Shirley Temple curls her father had been proud of and sometimes pruned to send snippets to relatives. In a convent twenty miles from the city Honor found a TV and a gigantic fridge. The Reverend Mother looked down into the fridge. She was fond of cold squid. A nearby town was not a ramshackle place but an American suburb. Palm trees, banks, benevolent-faced American men in panama hats. An American zinc company nearby. The girls who came to be taught were chocolate faced but still the children of the rich – the occasional chocolate-faced girl among them a young American with a tan. Honor that autumn found herself teaching Spenser to girls who watched the same TV programmes as the girls in the city she left. An American flag fluttered nearby and assured everyone, even the patrolling monkey-bodied teenage soldiers, that everything was all right. Such a dramatic geographical change, such a physical leap brought Honor in mind of Chris Gormley.

Chris Gormley had captivated her from the beginning, her long, layered blonde hair, her studious but easy manner. Honor was not in a position to publicly admire so she sometimes found herself insulting Chris. Only because she herself was bound and she was baulking at her own shackles. She cherished Chris though – Chris evoked the stolidity and generosity of her own background; she succeeded in suggesting an aesthetic from it and for this Honor was grateful – and when Chris went Honor knew she'd failed here, that she'd no longer have someone to banter with, to play word games with, and so left, hoping Chris one day would make a genius or a lover – for her sake – or both. Honor had been more than grateful to her though for participating in a debate with her and making one thing lucid to her – that occasionally you have to move on. So moving on for Honor meant travel, upheaval, and finding herself now beside a big Reverend Mother who as autumn progressed kept peering into a refrigerator bigger than herself.

A few months after she arrived in the convent however things had shifted emphasis; Honor was a regular sight in the afternoons after school throwing a final piece of cargo into a jeep and shooting – exploding – off in a cantankerous and erratic jeep with other nuns to a village thirty miles away. She'd become part of a cathectics corps. Beyond the American suburb was an American slum. Skeletal women with ink hair and big ink eyes with skeletal children lined the way. Honor understood why she'd always been drawn to Elizabethan Irish history. Because history recurs. For a moment in her mind these people were the victims of a British invasion. At first she was shy with the children. Unused to children. More used to teenage girls. But little boys graciously reached their hands to her and she relaxed, feeling better able to cope. The war was mainly in the mountains; sometimes it came near. But the children did not seem to mind. There was one child she became particularly fond of – Harry after Harry Belafonte – and he of her and one person she became drawn to, Brother Mark, a monk from Montana. He had blond hair, the colour of honey, balding in furrows. She wanted to put her fingers through it. Together they'd sit on a bench – the village was on an incline – on late afternoons that still looked like autumn, vineyards around, facing the Pacific which they could not see but knew was there from the Pacific sun hitting the clay of the vineyards, talking retrospectively of America. Did she miss America? No. She felt an abyss of contentment here among the little boys in white vests, with little brown arms already bulging with muscles. Brother Mark dressed in a white gown and one evening, intuiting her feelings for him – the fingers that wanted to touch the scorched, blue and red parts of his head – his hand reached from it to hers. To refrain from a relationship she volunteered for the mountains.

What she saw there would always be in her face, in her eyes. Hornet-like helicopters swooped on dark rivers of people in mountain-side forests and an American from San Francisco, Joseph Dinani, his long white hair like Moses's scrolls, hunched on the ground in an Indian poncho, reading the palms of refugees for money and food. He'd found his way through the forests of Central American in the early 1970s. There were bodies in a valley, many bodies, pregnant women, their stomachs rising out of the water like rhinoceroses bathing. Ever after that there'd be an alarm in her eyes and her right eyebrow was permanently estranged from her eye. She had to leave to tell someone but no one in authority for the moment wanted to know. The Americans were in charge and nothing too drastic could happen with the Americans around.

She threw herself into her work with the children. For some hours during the day she taught girls. The later hours, evening closing in in the hills, the mountains, she spent with the children. They became like her family. Little boys recognized the potential for comedy in her face and made her into a comedienne. In jeans and a blouse she jived with a boy as a fighter bomber went over. But the memory of what she'd seen in the mountains drove her on and made her every movement swifter. With this memory was the realization, consolidating all she felt about herself before leaving the school in the Midwest, that all her life she'd been running from something – boys

clanking chains in a suburb of a night-time Midwest city, hosts
of destroyers speeding through the beech shade of a fragment of
Elizabethan Irish history – and now they were catching up on
her. They had recognized her challenge. They had singled her
out. Her crime? To treat the poor like princes. She was just an
ordinary person now with blonde curly hair, a pale pretty face,
who happened to be American.

The Reverend Mother, a woman partly Venezuelan, partly
Brazilian, partly American, took at last to the doctrine of
liberation and a convent, always anarchistic, some nuns in
white, some in black, some in jeans and blouses, became more
anarchistic. She herself changed from black to white. She had
the television removed and replaced by a rare plant from Peru.
An American man in a white suit came to call on her and she
asked him loudly what had made him join the CIA and offered
him cooked octopus. Honor was producing a concert for harvest
festivities in her village that autumn.

There was a deluge of rats and mice – no one seemed sure
which – in the tobacco-coloured fields that autumn and an influx
of soldiers, young, rat-faced soldiers borne along, standing, on
front of jeeps. Rat eyes imperceptibly took in Honor. They had
caught up with her. A little girl in a blue dress crossed the fields,
tejacote apples upheld in the bottom of her dress. A little boy ran
to Honor. They were close at hand. At night when her fears were
most intense, sweat amassing on her face, she thought of Chris
Gormley, a girl at a school in the Midwest with whom she'd
shared a respite in her life, and if she said unkindnesses to her she
could say sorry now but that out of frustration comes the tree of
one's life. Honor's tree blossomed that autumn. Sometimes rain
poured. Sometimes the sky cheerily brightened. Pieces moved on
a chess table in a bar, almost of their own accord. In her mind
Honor heard a young soldier sing a song from an American
musical 'Out of my dreams and into your heart'.

The night of the concert squashes gleamed like moons in the
fields around the hall. In tight jeans, red check shirt, her curls
almost peroxide, Honor tightly sang a song into the microphone. Buddy Holly. 'You go your way and I'll go mine, now
and forever till the end of time.' A soldier at the back shouted an

obscenity at her. A little boy in front, in a grey T-shirt from Chicago, smiled his pleasure. In her mind was her father, his grey suit, the peace promised once when they were photographed together on a broad pavement of a city in the Midwest, that peace overturned now because it inevitably referred back to the turbulence which gave it, Irish-America, birth. And she saw the girl who in a way had brought her here. There was no panic in her, just a memory of an Elysium of broad, grey pavements and a liner trekking to Cobh, in County Cork. 'Yea, though I walk through the valley of the shadow of death, I will fear no evil: for thou art with me; thy rod and thy staff they comfort me.' In the morning they found her body with that of other nuns among ribbons of blood in a rubbish dump by a meeting of four roads. No one knew why they killed her because after the concert a young, almost Chinese-skinned soldier had danced with her under a yellow lantern that threw out scarlet patterns.

Afterwards Chris would wonder why her parents had not contacted her; perhaps the party with its barrage of phone calls had put up a barrier. But here, now, on the pavement, as the hearses passed, loaded with chrysanthemums and dahlias and carnations, she, this blonde, long-haired protégée of Sister Honor, could only be engulfed by the light of pumpkins which lit like candles in suburban gardens with dusk, by the lights of windows in high-rise blocks, apertures in catacombs in ancient Rome, by the flames which were emitted from factory chimneys and by the knowledge that a woman, once often harsh and forbidding, had been raised to the status of martyr and saint by a church which had continued since ancient Rome. An elderly lady in a blue mackintosh knelt on the pavement and pawed at a rosary. A negro lady beside Chris wept. But generally the crowd was silent, knowing that it had been their empire which had put these women to death and that now this city was receiving the bodies back among the flame of pumpkins, of windows, of rhythmically issuing factory fires, which scorched at the heart, turning it into a wilderness in horror and in awe.

Recovery

The coloured lights had still slashed into the black street the night her son had met with the accident. The lights strung up for summer in the town by the sea under the high mountain which seemed to capsize on the town – decorously – like a wave. Her son – Fiachra – she was told would never walk again after the accident. Some girls in their dance dresses had been squashed in around him. He'd been the most severely injured. It was three years on now and the doctors had proved right. Fiachra would never walk again. He'd been seventeen then. Just twenty now. In these three years the town had changed little but somehow it was difficult to sing into the microphone in their pub-cum-entertainment-lounge in summer. Still she managed – for his sake – clearing her voice and belting out a country and western number, her hair hennaed and curled after a secretive trip to Dublin. It was spring now and she wheeled Fiachra by an ocean, blue, not unlike her husband's eyes but totally unlike Fiachra's. His were green – like hers.

'Hello, how are you?' An old lady seemed to want to evaporate as she said hello to them, dipping her head to her right side. Broddie returned the greeting.

For three years she'd confronted many doctors, trying to stand erect and disdaining comfort herself; she traipsed through many hospitals. Her most recent journey to a hospital in Dublin had reminded her of a pilgrimage they used to make when she was a girl, on the flat, black bog, mainly women, tentatively, to a statue of the Virgin, surviving from the penal days, her form somewhat smudged like that of a corpse exhumed from a bog but still maintaining its features – the statue standing, hands

85

joined, head thrown back impervious to them, among a wild garden of bog-cotton. The pilgrims had approached like trappers about to snare a fox.

The journey to the hospital in Dublin, its final draining of energy from her, had reminded her of the way the long journey across the bog, its air of penitence, had drained her then. Instead of a statue of the Virgin, at the end of the journey to Dublin, had been a Sri Lankan doctor. Fiachra was home now. And together they applauded the sea. But he would never, ever, be the boy who walked with her among the Goyas in the National Gallery in Dublin a few years beforehand, his black hair like the hair in a Goya painting, his face, long, heavy, like that of Goya himself. And yet she held out hope for something. What? Then, when she'd been a girl, they'd trudge to the statue of the Virgin – bombs had been generously falling on Liverpool – expecting something, not so much a miracle as a message. Only the aged could decipher the messages then and a nearly blind lady – a Mrs Gormley who wrapped nylon stockings around her neck for warmth – could see perfectly again.

The little town with its outposts of German factories now had all but killed any such expectation of the amazing in her. But of late her thoughts, unwillingly, had been turned to pilgrimage again.

'Look Mammy there's a boat on the sea,' Broddie refrained from cynicism; a rich German. 'Mammy, look at those rock flowers. Remember the way you used to say the first flowers of the year on the beach reminded you of the way Daddy proposed to you. On a big rock on the beach after he'd removed your high heels and baptized your toes in a rock pool.'

Years of marriage, years of motherhood had made Broddie ripe for pilgrimage; she was aged now. Much as she'd tried to look young. She'd let her other children fly around the world. Before other people in these parts had done so. It was the anarchy of their household which in part had caused Fiachra's accident. She'd allowed him to go dancing to a last marquee of the season when he should have been in bed.

Yes, her face in a rock pool now would show the face of an old woman. One of these days she'd go to the bog.

'Mammy, why don't you sing a song.' She began 'Black Velvet Band'. Then she realized how ridiculous she must sound, an older woman throwing out a pub song by the sea and she stopped. Fiachra did not say anything. When she got home she saw her face enshrined in a scarf in a mirror and identified all the signs of recent decay and uncertainty.

Fiachra wheeled himself by the ocean; he spun along by the spring blue of the sea. But his face still had the look, despite his Olympian fortitude, that life had been taken from it. That death had occurred in it many times over. Broddie prepared for the bog.

With each piece of clothing she put on for the journey, dowdy clothes, a mustard-coloured coat, years peeled away, wallpaper drooping off walls.

The morning was grey, mellifluous. She slipped away furtively; as one of the homosexuals who were said to manifest themselves at the town lavatory now. Her head was wrapped in a white scarf with a pattern of green pound notes. Someone mindful of money had given it to her. The previous night Fiachra had barked something at his father. Tempers were cobweb-frail in the house. Broddie marched into the bog.

When she'd been a girl it had been a different world; there'd been different colours. Girls stood opposite men on the dancefloor in yellow ochre and brown clothes. Young men and young women had clapped one another's hands in strange dances. Women in red petticoats had descended from the mountain when disaster had occurred there and had approached the statue of the Virgin in the bog. It had been strange that she, the most ambitious girl in the town, had married a local young man and stayed here.

But Ollie Hanamy, his gauche way of standing on the dancehall floor, his black suit, jacket loose on an open white shirt, the poems he'd promised despite his publican's trade, had captivated her. She had imagined the poems at some point would deliver her out of here. No poems came. A profusion of offspring though. They in time had taken off to New York, San Francisco, Paris, London. All except Fiachra, the youngest. And now the most ultimate, the most imaginatively untenable calamity had befallen on him; he, her youngest, was crippled for life. She had tried many times to rationalize it. He had tried to rationalize it. She could see it in him. She'd wanted many times to reach to him and make it easier. But together they could only trespass on the area between them, a border of grief. And this grief sent her back, made her journey back, to the blue of the sky and the sea around when she was young and women in red petticoats came from the mountains for the Good Friday mortifications. Christ gagged and blindfolded on the cross in the church.

It had been this haphazard ocean, the blue of the sea on fine days, that she took with her as a friend, as a fellow conspirator through her marriage. And with this benevolence was an image which saved her from many days of despair, the image of a cathedral her husband told her about when they married, a cathedral on a hill in France, that had warded off bombs and survived the war. The cathedral was reputed to be magnificent, dark and grey. She'd never go there. She'd allowed her children to make trips there instead of her. She'd just sung, dolled her hair up, and sung in her later years, thinking of cathedrals in France and alleyways traced with virginia creeper, red and varicose with autumn, which led to them, old stooped men, black berets shoved on their heads like punctured footballs, eddying on these alleyways.

Fiachra often looked like a cathedral himself, his broad shoulders, black hair, heavy face, the black leather jacket he twitched from side to side in now. But if he was a cathedral now he was a broken one and her one prayer this morning was that the pieces could be picked up, scooped up, and somehow miraculously strung together again.

The sky was pearly now, a bird assailed it, flying low and then suddenly rising, issuing a wet trickle of protest. Rain held back. Yellow flowers were coming into being – what were their names – Broddie had lost the lore of the bog.

Suddenly she realized she was not alone in the bog; from the direction of the Virgin a figure took shape and approached, slowly. When the figure was near Broddie could see it was a woman in black. The woman did not come near Broddie but passed her – at a distance. Broddie did not recognize her. A woman from the country maybe. A scarf on her head, her head dipped and engrossed. When they were parallel to one another it was as if they both stopped, in solidarity with one another's requests, and it seemed to Broddie, that for that strange, dramatic, inexplicable moment, heather sweeping between them, that it was not now but hundreds of years ago and that they were two figures in a world which sustained itself only on prayers. Time had taken them by the hand and brought them back to a stage in history when the bog had been a last shelter and even the Virgin had been a refugee in one of its black crannies. The Virgin still clung to the soil of that subterfuge and had brought them both here this morning. The other woman did not look at Broddie but fully understood, allowed for, her presence. Then she was gone and Broddie felt a bleakness she'd felt as a child when deserted by parents. She headed on, knowing that the space around the Virgin had to be redefined again by her and all the pain of pilgrims who'd come here be raised again and reckoned with.

She was entering a bleak classroom in a national school long ago. There was little for comfort and a teacher waiting to admonish her. Broddie stood at last in front of the Virgin and began her incoherent prayer.

The Virgin was a small stubby thing. She had grown smaller with time and in front of her Broddie felt thin and mean and avaricious. The weather was somehow suddenly colder. Broddie shuddered. She enumerated again for herself the events and feelings surrounding the accident. It had been a Friday night, beginning to be wet. Black on the pavement. She'd run to a reflection of a coloured light thinking it to be blood. There'd been the helicopter to Dublin. The waiting to see if he was going to live. The cigarettes. The prayers. Her husband even made up a poem. Her children had come back and then they'd left, one by one, leaving her, when Fiachra at last came home, with the excrement. She'd become mean, fossilized. She'd smoked a lot. Dyed her hair a lot. And then one day, broke down by the sea, when no one could be spectator to her breakdown. She'd tried to tear her dyed curls out but then abandoned the effort and went home, resuming her duties with Fiachra. Now she faced the Virgin, a reflection of her thin self, got no satisfaction from her, and somehow cursing her as you would a neighbour who was both ally and tormentor, reduced from high language and lofty ideas to a stream of gutter words, she turned away, feeling the indignity and lack of grace of her own movements.

Fiachra asked his father to help him with a change of clothes that afternoon. He wheeled himself out. By the sea, on the promenade, he stopped for a moment, looking to the sea, then spun himself on. As he spun the wheelchair accelerated itself to its own motion. In Fiachra's mind too was the night of the accident as had been there many times before, the lamppost looking in like a person, the moment before unconsciousness and lifetime injury.

The hospital in the big town in his county, the hospitals in Dublin, the whiteness of his casts, the blood his veins had imbibed, a heartbeat of its own, the visitors, the new world he found beyond the real world, a world on the moon of his mind, the new territory he journeyed to, the return home, a nun from the convent where he'd gone to primary school who seemed to understand everything, the rainbows on the bog, the rainbows on the sea, the little humped bridge over the stream where he got various members of his family to stop with him. That bridge had been adolescence for him. Standing there with girls. Now adolescence and a certain life was gone. But he insisted on being taken to that bridge because of its eccentric malformation. He'd already been conspiring to go on living. A huge cloud blanketed the sky now. Rain was expected. There'd been blue for a while in the afternoon. Now that cloud was going to blanket out the blue.

But both the grey and the blue were indecisive and in the jostle between them rainbows, colours, diamonds sprung up on pools among symmetries of rocks on the beach. There'd been a cathedral once his mother had told him about, in France, which had survived bombs and war, which had magically fenced itself off from bombs and war and now that cathedral was in his mind as it often had been before but whereas before, as a child, it had troubled him that he could only see grey walls and ramparts of this cathedral now stained-glass windows began in it, taking their colours from the sparks of light in the rock pools, beginning, a stream of them, an escalator between the rock pools and the imaginary cathedral, bearing them along. The process continued. A colour here. A colour there until the cathedral was at last completed with flashing, iridescent, many and finely coloured stained-glass windows. There were saints and soldiers in them although you could not make them out because they were back to front so Fiachra entered the cathedral and in his wheelchair, stopped, and looked to the rose window.

The cathedral was cold, chilly even, but with a freshness which had survived since the Middle Ages. In the dark there was just one window now for the boy in the wheelchair, a communication between him and the rose window which invited in light and sent it to him in signals. The boy and the window conversed. Then the boy left and he was back on the promenade with the rain falling.

Broddie had caught the beginning of the rain as she reached the end of the bog, her figure looking tired, her feet squelching into wet now. When she got home she removed her wet scarf and her wet coat and as she was doing so, in the darkened hallway, by the hall stand mirror, Fiachra entered.

She turned to him. His limbs – feet, arms – his torso were just the same – she started down there – but with the collar of his black leather jacket open she could see he'd put on a tie with his shirt – or had it put on – for the first time since his accident, a broad deep green jade tie with a plush orange summer shirt that had skirted his incongruously bony arms in summer once. And above the shirt and tie, inviting her – the Virgin flashed in her mind not as she'd seen her today but as she'd seen her in summer long ago, rubbed by bog-cotton – was a face that was totally different from the one she'd become accustomed to but was that of the boy she chaperoned through the Goyas in the National Gallery once. Black hair, pale skin, alive, entreating gentle eyes. His body might have been dead but above that body, shocking Broddie, was the mound of a head, the black, irregular, restless head of an artist.

A Marriage in the Country

She burned down half her house early that summer and killed her husband. He'd been caught upstairs. It was something she'd often threatened to do, burn the house down, and when she did it she did it quietly, in a moment of silent, reflective despair. She had not known he'd been upstairs. She'd put a broom in the stove and then tarred the walls with the fire. The flames had quickly explored the narrow stairway. A man, twenty years older than her, had been burned alive, caught when snoozing. Magella at his funeral seemed charred herself, her black hair, her pale, almost sucrose skin. She'd stooped, in numbed penitence. There was a nebulous, almost incandesced way her black curls took form from her forehead as there was about all the Scully girls. They made an odd band of women there, all the Scully girls, most of them respectably married. Magella was the one who'd married a dozy publican whose passion in life had been genealogy and whose ambition seemed incapacitated by this passion. She'd had a daughter by him. Gráinne. That girl was taken from her that summer and sent to relatives in Belfast. Magella was not interned in a mental hospital. The house was renovated. The pub reopened. People supposed that the shock of what she'd done had cured her and in a genuinely solicitous way they thought that working in the pub, chattering to the customers, would be better for her than an internment in a mental hospital. Anyway there was something very final about internment in a mental hospital at that time in Ireland. They gave her a reprieve. At the end of that summer Boris came to the village.

Stacks of hay were piled up in the fields near the newly

opened garage outside the village which he came to manage, little juggling acts of hay in merrily rolling and intently bound fields. All was smallness and precision here. This was Laois. An Ascendancy demesne. The garage was on the top of a hill where the one, real, village street ended, and located at a point where the fields seemed about to deluge the road. The one loss of sobriety in the landscape and heaviness and a very minor one. Boris began his career as garage manager by putting up flags outside the garage, and bunting, an American, an Italian, a French, a Spanish, a German and an Irish flag. He was half-Russian and he'd been raised in an orphanage in County Wexford in the south-eastern tip of Ireland.

Boris Cleary was thin, nervously thin, black-haired, a blackness smoothing the parts of his face which he'd shaved and the very first thing Magella noticed about him, on coming close, under the bunting, was that there was a smell from the back of his neck, as from wild flowers lost in the deep woods which lay in the immediate surroundings of the village. A rancid, asking smell. A smell which asked you to investigate its bearer. Magella, drawn by the rancid smell from the back of a nervous, thin neck, sought further details. She asked Boris about his Russianness which was already, after a few weeks, a rampant legend over her counter. His father had been a Russian sailor, his mother a Wexford prostitute; he'd been dumped on the Sisters of Mercy. They had christened him and one particular nun had reared him, cackling all the time at this international irony, calling him 'little Stalin'. Boris had emerged, his being, his presence in the world, had emerged from an inchoate night on a ship in the port of Wexford town.

How a September night, the last night like neon on the gold of the cornfields, led so rapidly to the woods partly surrounding the village they later lost track of; winter conversations in the pub, glasses of whiskey, eventually glasses of whiskey shared, both their mouths going to a glass, like a competition – a series of reciprocal challenges. Eventually, all the customers gone one night as they tended to be gone when Magella and Boris got involved in conversation, their lips met. An older woman, ascribed a demon by some, began having an affair with a young, slackly put-together man.

The woods in early summer was the culminative platform for their affair. These woods which were in fact a kind of garden for bygone estates. Always in the woods, oases, you'd find a garden house – a piece of concrete – a Presbyterian, a Methodist, a Church of Ireland chapel. Much prayer had been done on these estates. Laois had particularly been a county in bondage. Now rhododendrons fulminated and frothed all over the place. And there were berries to admire, right from the beginning of the summer. They found a particular summer house where they made love on the cold, hard, almost penitential floor and soon this was the only place where they made love, their refuge.

In September, just over a year after Boris had come to the village, they got a taxi and visited Magella's daughter in Belfast. She lived off the Falls Road, in a house beside a huge advertisement on a railway bridge for the *Irish Independent*. Gráinne dressed in an odious brown, convent uniform. She had long black hair. She looked at Boris. From the look in her eyes Magella afterwards realized she'd fallen in love with Boris at that meeting.

What were they flaunting an affair for? At first they were flaunting it so openly no one believed it was happening. Such things didn't happen in Laois in the 1950s. People presumed that the young Russian had taken a priestly interest in the older possessed woman. And when they brought their affair to Belfast, Boris in a very natty dark suit and in a tie of shining dark blue, a gaggle of relatives thought that there was something comic going on, that Magella had got a clown to chaperone her and prevent her from acts of murderous madness. They brought glasses of orange on to the street for the pair – it was a very sunny day – and oddly enough there was a spark of bunting on the street, the ordination of a local priest recently celebrated. A bulbous-cheeked, Amazon-breasted woman spluttered out a comment. 'Sure he reminds me of the King of England.' She was referring to the king who'd resigned, the only member of royalty respected in Nationalist Belfast.

But behind the screen of all the presumptions – and it was a kind of smokescreen – something very intense, very carnal, very complex was going on. Magella was discovering her flesh for the first time and Boris was in a way discovering a mother. She'd always been the licentious one in her family but flailing her flesh around cornfields at night when she'd been young brought her no real pleasure. In the carnality, in love-making now, she'd found lost worlds of youth and lost – yes, inchoate – worlds of Russia. She was able to travel to Boris's origins and locate a very particular house. It was a house in a wood away from the dangers of the time. In this house she put Boris's forebears. In this house, in her sexual fantasies, she made love to Boris, his forebears gone and only they, random lovers, left in it, away from the dangers and the onslaught of the time. There was a tumultuous excitement about being lovers in a house in a wood with many dangers outside the borders of that wood. There was a titillation, a daring, and even a brusqueness about it. But those dangers eventually slipped their moorings in the world outside the wood.

Early in the second summer of their affair someone saw them making love in the summer house. A little boy. Tremulous though he later was about the event he was matter of fact enough to wait for a good view of Magella's heavy white thighs. He was the butcher's son. A picture was soon contrived all over the village, Magella and Boris in an act of love which had a Bolshevik ferocity. Killing your husband was one thing but making love to a young Russian was another. Within the month Magella was in a mental hospital.

The funny thing was that she'd had a premonition that all this was going to happen some weeks before the little boy saw them. Fondling some budding elderberries in the woods she remarked to Boris, looking back at the visible passage they'd made through the woods, that they, she and him, reminded her of the legendary Irish lovers, Diarmaid and Gráinne, who'd fled a king into the woods, feeding on berries. They'd invested Irish berries with a sense of doomed carnality, the berries which had sustained them, right down to the last morsels of late autumn. Here in these woods many of the berries had been sown as parts of gardens and it was difficult to distinguish the wild berries from the descendants of a Protestant bush – the loganberry, redcurrant, raspberry. These woods had been a testing ground for horticulture and parts of the woods had been cultivated at random, leaving a bed of mesmeric flowers, an apple tree among the wildness. Diarmaid and Gráinne would have had a ball here Magella said. But for her and Boris the climate was already late autumn when the trees were withered of berries. Their days were up. She remembered the chill she'd felt at national school when the teacher had come to that part of the story of Diarmaid and Gráinne, reading it from a book which had an orange cover luminous as warm blood.

Boris tried to call on her in the mental hospital. He was wearing a suit. But there was a kind of consternation among nuns and nurses when they saw him – they weren't sure what to do – he stood, shouldering criminality, for a few minutes in the waiting room and then he turned on his heels and left. But there was a despatch from his childhood here. A statue of a frigid white Virgin as there'd been in the lounge of the orphanage. Magella had entered the house, all grey and fragmented with statues of Mary like falling crusts of snowflakes, of his childhood.

The years went by and the garage prospered. Gráinne came down from Belfast, having graduated from the convent. Her keen eye on Boris at their first meeting in Belfast led now, after all these years, to a romance. There'd been an unmitigated passion in between. Gráinne started walking out the roads with Boris, her hair cut short and the dresses of a middle-aged woman on her, dour, brown, her figure too becoming somewhat lumpy and, in a middle-aged way, becoming acquiescent. She was very soon linking Boris's arm. She and Boris went to see her mother who sat in a room in the mental hospital, a very quiet Rapunzel but without the long, golden hair of course. Boris, armed with Magella's daughter, was allowed in now. He approached Magella, who was seated, as if there'd been no carnality between them, as if he couldn't remember it, as though this woman was his mother and had been in a mother relationship with him. The affair with her, memory of it, had, in this Catholic village, evacuated his mind. Beside Gráinne he looked like a businessman, as someone who'd been operated on and had his aura of passion removed. He drooped, a lazily held puppet. There was a complete change in him, a complete reorganization of the state of his being, a change commensurate with collectivization in Stalinist Russia. Only very tiny shards of his former being remained, littered on the railway tracks of it, the thoroughfare of it. He didn't so much deny Magella as hurt her with an impotent perception of her. At the core of her love-making with him there'd been a child searching for his mother and now, the memory of passion gone, there was only the truth of his findings. A mother. The mother of a weedy son at that. The rancid smell at the back of his neck had turned to a sickly-sweet one. But Magella still ached for the person who would be revived as soon as she got her hands on Boris again. That person tremored somewhere inside Boris, at the terribleness of her ability.

The romance between Boris and Gráinne lapsed and Gráinne went off to work in a beauty parlour in Bradford where relatives of her father lived. A few months after her departure Boris – there'd been tiffs between them – repented of his irascibility in the weeks before her decision to leave and he went looking for her. He ended up beside a slime heap in Bradford, a house beside a slime heap, exiled Irish people. The beauty parlour was a few streets away. People in Bradford called Boris Paddy which further confused his sense of identity and he went home without resolving things with Gráinne to find Magella out of the mental hospital and having reopened the pub which Gráinne had tentatively opened for a while. Everything was ripe for a confrontation between them but Magella kept a quietness, even a dormancy in that pub for months until one night she raged out to the garage, wielding a broom, a like instrument to that of her husband's death. He met her at the door of his little house alongside the garage which was closed for the night. 'You scut,' she said. 'You took two dogs from me once and never gave them back.' True, Boris had taken two ginger-coloured, chalk cocker spaniels for his mantelpiece on the condition he'd return them when he found something suitable for the mantelpiece himself. 'I want them back,' she said. He let her in. The dogs were there. She stood in front of him, not looking at the dogs. Where there had been black hair there was now mainly a smoke of grey. She stood in front of him, silently, broom inoffensively by her side, as if to show him the wreck of her being, a wreck caused by involvement with him. 'Come down for a drink some night,' she said and quietly went off.

He did go down for a drink in her pub. He fiddled with drinks on the counter. Then Gráinne came back and Magella burned the whole house down, everything, leaving only a charred wreck of a house. She was put back into the mental hospital. There'd been no money left in the bank. Everything was squandered now and everything had been amiss anyway before Magella had burned the house down. Maybe that's why she'd burned the house down. But this wreck, this cavity in the street was her statement. It was her statement before Boris and Gráinne announced plans for marriage.

What Gráinne did not know when she was earnestly proposed marriage to was that Boris and Magella had slipped away together for a honeymoon of their own in Bray, County Wicklow, the previous June. They stayed in a cascade of a hotel by the sea. The mountains, Bray Head were frills on the sea. The days were very blue. Woman walked dogs, desultory Russian émigrés in pinks, purples, with hats pushed down over their ears. You never saw their faces. Boris and Magella slept in the same room but in separate beds. There were rhododendrons on hills just over Bray and among the walks on those hills. Boris explained to Magella that she was the real woman in his life, at first a carnal one, then a purified, sublimated one. She'd been the one he'd been looking for. It was difficult for Magella to take this, that physical love was over in her life, but there was affirmation with the pain when she eventually burned down the house, on hearing of Boris's imminent marriage to Gráinne. She'd achieved something.

In Bray before they used to go to sleep Boris would light a candle in the room and sit up in bed thinking. 'What are you thinking of?' she asked. But he'd never answered. Nuns in Wexford, gulls streaming over an orphanage, poised to drop for crusts of bread on a grey playing area, sailors on the sea, migrations on foot by railroads in Russia, heavy sun on people in rags, a grandmother pulling a child by the hand, the only remaining member of her family.

'You've got to go through one thing to get to the other,' Boris said sagely as he sat up in bed one night, the lights still on, impeccable pyjamas of navy and white stripes on him which revealed a bush of the acrid black hair on his chest, he staring ahead, zombie-like.

In this statement he'd meant he'd gone through physical love with Magella to fish up a dolorous, muted ikon of a Virgin, of the untouchable but all-protecting woman. To get this holy protection from a woman you had to make her untouchable, sacred. For the rest of his life Magella would provide the source of sanity, of resolve, of belief in his life. She was the woman who'd rescued him from the inchoate Wexford night.

Magella was, of course, pleased to hear this but still restive. She did not sleep well that night. She longed, despite that statement, to have Boris, his nimble legs and arms, his pale well of a crotch, in her bed.

The marriage took place in July the following year. There was a crossroads dance the night before a mile or two outside the village. Rare enough in Ireland at that time, even in West Kerry and in Connemara, they still happened in this backwater of County Laois. People stepped out beside a few items of a funfair, a few coloured lights strung up. An epic, a tumultous smell of corn came from the fields. A melodion played the tune 'Slievenamban'. 'My love, o my love, will I ne' er see you again, in the valley of Slievenamban?' Lovers sauntered through the corn. Magella was packing her things in the mental hospital to attend the wedding the following day.

On their second last day in Bray, by the sea, he'd suddenly hugged her and she saw all the mirth again in his face and all the dark in his hair. An old man nearby, his eye on them, quickly wound up a machine to play some music. There was a picture of Sorrento on a funfair caravan, pale blue lines on the yellow ochre caravan, cartoon Italian mountains, cartoon packed Italian houses, cartoon, operatic waves. Magella had looked to the sea, beyond the straggled funfair, and seen the blue in the sea which was tangible, which was ecstatic.

Magella danced with Boris at the wedding reception. She was wearing a brown suit and a brown hat lent to her by her sister in Tihelly, County Offaly. She looked like an alcoholic beverage, an Irish cream liqueur. Or so a little boy who'd come to the wedding thought. She danced with him in a room where ten pound notes, twenty pound notes and, of course, many five pound notes were pinned on the walls as was the custom at weddings in Ireland. The little boy had come a long way that morning. His granny, on the other side of his family whom he called on on the way, in her little house, had given him a box of chocolates which looked like a navy limousine. He still had it now as he watched Boris and Magella dance, the couple, a serenity between them, an understanding. They'd been looking for different things from one another, their paths had crossed, they'd gone different ways but in this moment they created a total communion, a total marriage, an understanding that only a child could intuit and carry away with him, enlightened, the notes on the walls becoming Russian notes with pictures of Tsars and dictators and people who'd changed epochs on them, the walls burning in a terrible fire in the child's mind until only a note or two was left, a face or two, sole reminders of an enraptured moment in history.

At such moments the imagination begins and someone else, someone who did not live through the events, remembers and, later, counts the pain.

A little boy walked away from the wedding, box of chocolates still under his arm, not wanting to look back at the point where a woman was dragged away, screaming, at a certain hour, to a solitary room in a mental hospital.

Years later he returned, long after Magella's death in the mental hospital, to the woods, at the time of year when rhododendrons spread there. He bent and picked up a decapitated tiara of rhododendron. There was a poster for Paris in the village, a Chinese restaurant run by a South Korean, a late night fish-and-chip takeaway. The garage was still open at the top of the village. The only change was that Boris had put up a Russian flag among the others. It was his showpiece. He'd gotten it from the Legion of Mary in Kilkenny who'd put on a show about imprisoned cardinals behind the Iron Curtain. But it was his pride. It demonstrated, apart from his roots, the true internationalism of the garage. There were no boundaries here. A bald man, lots of children scampering around him for years, would come out to fill your car and his face would tell you these things, a brown, anaemic work coat on him, a prosperous but also somewhat cowed grin on his face.

At her funeral in 1959 Boris had carried lilies, and there, in the graveyard, thought of his visit to Bradford, the exiled Irish there, a cowed, depressed people, the legacy of history, and of the woman who'd tried to overthrow that legacy, for a while. He'd put the lilies on the grave, Magella's lover, no one denying that day the exact place of the grief in his heart.

Everybody walked away except the boy and Boris and then Boris walked away, but first looking at the boy, almost in annoyance, as if to say, you have no right to intrude on these things, flashing back his black hair and throwing a boyish, almost a rival's look from his black eyes which were scarred and vinegary and blazingly alive from tears. In those eyes was the wound, the secret, and the boy looked at it, unreproached by it.

Years later he returned to find that there was no museum to that wound, only a few brightly painted houses, a ramshackle cramming of modernity. He took his car and drove out by the garage and the bunting and the flags to the fields where you could smell the first, premature coming of the epic, all-consuming, wound-oblivionizing harvest.

Our mad aunts, the young man thought, our mad selves.

Lady of Laois, ikon from this incumbent, serf-less, but none the less, I expect, totally Russian story-book blinding harvest, pray for the night-sea, neon spin-drift, jukebox-beacon café wanderer.

Ties

I

The Forty Steps led nowhere. They were grey and wide, shadowed at the sides by creeper and bush. In fact it was officially declared by Patsy Fogarthy that there were forty-four steps. These steps were erected by an English landlord in memorial to some doubtful subject. A greyhound, a wife? If you climbed them you had a view of the recesses of the woods and the places where Patsy Fogarthy practised with his trombone. Besides playing – in a navy uniform – in the brass band Patsy Fogarthy was my father's shop assistant. While the steps were dark grey the counter in my father's shop was dark and fathomless. We lived where the town men's Protestant society had once been and that was where our shop was too. And still is. Despite the fact my father is dead. My father bought the house, built the shop from nothing – after a row with a brother with whom he shared the traditional family grocery-cum-bar business. Patsy Fogarthy was my father's first shop assistant. They navigated waters together. They sold silk ties, demonstrating them carefully to country farmers.

Patsy Fogarthy was from the country, had a tremendous welter of tragedy in his family – which always was a point of distinction – deranged aunts, a paralysed mother. We knew that Patsy's house – cottage – was in the country. We never went there. It was just a picture. And in the cottage in turn in my mind were many pictures – paintings, embroideries by a prolific local artist who took to embroidery when she was told she was destined to die from leukaemia. Even my mother had one of her works. A bowl of flowers on a firescreen. From his inception as part of our household it seems that Patsy had allied himself towards me. In fact he'd been my father's assistant from before I was born. But he dragged me on walks, he described linnets to me, he indicated ragwort, he seated me on wooden benches in the hall outside town opposite a line of sycamores as he puffed into his trombone, as his fat stomach heaved into it. Patsy had not always been fat. That was obvious. He'd been corpulent, not fat. 'Look,' he said one day on the avenue leading to the Forty Steps – I was seven – 'A blackbird about to burst into song.'

Patsy had burst into song once. At a St Patrick's night concert. He sang 'Patsy Fagan'. Beside a calendar photograph of a woman at the back of our shop he did not sing for me but recited poetry. 'The Ballad of Athlone.' The taking of the bridge of Athlone by the Williamites in 1691 had dire consequences for this area. It implanted it forevermore with Williamites. It directly caused the Irish defeat at Aughrim. Patsy lived in the shadow of the hills of Aughrim. Poppies were the consequence of battle. There were balloons of defeat in the air. Patsy Fogarthy brought me a gift of mushrooms once from the fields of Aughrim.

Patsy had a bedding of blackberry curls about his cherubic face; he had cherubic lips and smiled often; there was a snowy sparkle in his deep-blue eyes. Once he'd have been exceedingly good-looking. When I was nine his buttocks slouched obesely. Once he'd have been as the man in the cigarette advertisements. When I was nine on top of the Forty Steps he pulled down his jaded trousers as if to pee, opened up his knickers and exposed his gargantuan balls. Delicately I turned away. The same year he tried to put the same penis in the backside of a drummer in the brass band, or so trembling, thin members of the Legion of Mary vouched. Without a murmur of a court case Patsy was expelled from town. The boy hadn't complained. He'd been caught in the act by a postman who was one of the church's most faithful members in town. Patsy Fogarthy crossed the Irish Sea, leaving a trail of mucus after him.

2

I left Ireland for good and all 11 October, 1977. There'd been many explanations for Patsy's behaviour: an aunt who used to have fits, throwing her arms about like seven snakes; the fact he might really have been of implanted Williamite stock. One way or the other he'd never been quite forgotten, unmentioned for a while, yes, but meanwhile the ecumenical movement had revived thoughts of him.

My mother attended a Protestant service in St Matthias's church in 1976. As I left home she pressed a white, skeletal piece of paper into my hands. The address of a hospital where Patsy Fogarthy was now incarcerated. The message was this 'Visit him. We are now Christian (we go to Protestant services) and if not forgiven he can have some alms.' It was now one could go back that made people accept him a little. He'd sung so well once. He smiled so cheerily. And sure wasn't there the time he gave purple Michaelmas daisies to the dying and octogenarian and well-nigh crippled Mrs Connaughton (she whose husband left her and went to America in 1927).

I did not bring Patsy Fogarthy purple Michaelmas daisies. In the house I was staying in in Battersea there were marigolds. Brought there regularly by myself. Patsy was nearby in a Catholic hospital in Wandsworth. Old clay was dug up. Had my mother recently been speaking to a relative of his? A casual conversation on the street with a country woman. Anyway this was the task I was given. There was an amber, welcoming light in Battersea. Young deer talked to children in Battersea Park. I crept around Soho like an escaped prisoner. I knew there was something connecting then and now, yes, a piece of paper, connecting the far-off, starched days of childhood to an adulthood which was confused, desperate but determined to make a niche away from family and all friends that had ensued from a middle-class Irish upbringing. I tiptoed up bare wooden stairs at night, scared of waking those who'd given me lodging. I tried to write to my mother and then I remembered the guilty conscience on her face.

Gas works burgeoned into the honey-coloured sky, oblivious of the landscape inside me, the dirty avenue cascading on the Forty Steps.

'Why do you think they built it?'

'To hide something.'

TIES

'Why did they want to hide something?'
'Because people don't want to know about some things.'
'What things?'
Patsy had shrugged, a fawn coat draped on his shoulders that day.
'Patsy, I'll never hide anything.'
There'd been many things I'd hidden. A girlfriend's abortion. An image of a little boy inside myself, a blue and white striped T-shirt on him. The mortal end of a relationship with a girl. Desire for my own sex. Loneliness. I'd tried to hide the loneliness, but Dublin, city of my youth, had exposed loneliness like a neon at evening. I'd hidden a whole part of my childhood, the 1950s, but hitting London took them out of the bag. Irish pubs in London, their jukeboxes, united the 1950s with the 1970s with a kiss of a song. 'Patsy Fagan'. Murky waters wheezed under a mirror in a pub lavatory. A young man in an Italian-style duffle coat, standing erect, eddied into a little boy being tugged along by a small fat man.
'Patsy what is beauty?'
'Beauty is in the eye of the beholder.'
'But what is it?'
He looked at me. 'Pretending we're father and son now.'
I brought Patsy Fogarthy white carnations. It was a sunny afternoon early in November. I'd followed instructions on a piece of paper. Walking into the demesne of the hospital I perceived light playing in a bush. He was not surprised to see me. He was a small, fat, bald man in pyjamas. His face and his baldness were a carnage of reds and purples. Little wriggles of grey hair stood out. He wore maroon and red striped pyjamas. He gorged me with a look. 'You're – ' I did not want him to say my name. He took my hand. There was death in the intimacy. He was in a hospital for the mad. He made a fuss of being grateful for the flowers. 'How's Georgina?' He called my mother by her first name. 'And Bert?' My father was not yet dead. It was as if he was charging them with something. Patsy Fogarthy, our small-town Oscar Wilde, reclined in pyjamas on a chair against the shimmering citadels of Wandsworth. A white nun infrequently scurried in to see to some man in the corridor. 'You

made a fine young man.' 'It was the band I missed most.' 'Them were the days.' In the middle of snippets of conversation – he sounded not like an Irish bank clerk, aged though and more gravel-voiced – I imagined the tableau of love, Patsy with a young boy. 'It was a great old band. Sure you've been years out of the place now. What age are ye? Twenty-six. Do you have a girlfriend? The English girls will be out to grab you now.' A plane noisily slid over Wandsworth. We simultaneously looked at it. An old, swede-faced man bent over a bedside dresser. 'Do ya remember me? I used to bring you on walks.' Of course I said. Of course. 'It's not true what they said about us. Not true. They're all mad. They're all lunatics. How's Bert?' Suddenly he started shouting at me. 'You never wrote back. You never wrote back to my letters. And all the ones I sent you.' More easy-voiced he was about to return the flowers until he suddenly avowed. 'They'll be all right for Our Lady. They'll be all right for Our Lady.' Our Lady was a white statue, over bananas and pears, by his bed.

3

It is hot summer in London. Tiger lilies have come to my door. I'd never known Patsy had written to me. I'd never received his letters of course. They'd curdled in my mother's hand. All through my adolescence. I imagined them filing in, never to be answered. I was Patsy's boy. More than the drummer lad. He had betrothed himself to me. The week after seeing him, after being virtually chased out of the ward by him, with money I'd saved up in Dublin, I took a week's holiday in Italy. The *trattorias* of Florence in November illumined the face of a young man who'd been Patsy Fogarthy before I'd been born. It's now six years on and that face still puzzles me, the face I saw in Florence, a young man with black hair, and it makes a story that solves a lot of mystery for me. There's a young man with black hair in a scarlet tie but it's not Patsy. It's a young man my father met in London in 1939, the year he came to study tailoring. Perhaps now it's the summer and the heat and the picture of my father on the wall – a red and yellow striped tie on him – and my illimitable estrangement from family but this city creates a series of ikons this summer. Patsy is one of them. But the sequence begins in the summer of 1939.

Bert ended up on the wide pavements of London in the early summer of 1939. He came from a town in the Western Midlands of Ireland whose wide river had scintillated at the back of town before he left and whose handsome façades radiated with sunshine. There were girls left behind that summer and cricket matches. Bert had decided on the tailoring course after a row with an older brother with whom he'd shared the family grocery-cum-bar business. The family house was one of the most sizeable on the street. Bert had his eyes on another house to buy now. He'd come to London to forge a little bit of independence from family for himself and in so doing he forwent some of the pleasures of the summer. Not only had he left the green cricket fields by the river but he had come to a city that exhaled news bulletins. He was not staying long.

He strolled into a cavern of death for behind the cheery faces of London that summer was death. Bert would do his course in Cheapside and not linger. Badges pressed against military lapels, old dishonours to Ireland. Once Bert had taken a Protestant girl out. They sailed in the bumpers at the October fair together. That was the height of his forgiveness for England. He did not consider playing cricket a leaning to England. Cricket was an Irish game, pure and simple, as could be seen from its popularity in his small, Protestant-built town.

Living was not easy for Bert in London; an Irish landlady – she was from Armagh, a mangy woman – had him. Otherwise the broth of his accent was rebuffed. He stooped a little under English disdain, but his hair was still orange and his face ruddy in fragments. By day Bert travailed; a dusty, dark cubicle. At evenings he walked. It was the midsummer which made him raise his head a little.

Twilight rushing over the tops of the trees at the edge of Hyde Park made him think of his dead parents, Galway people. He was suddenly both proud of and abstracted by his lineage. A hat was vaunted by his red hands on his waist. One evening, as perfumes and colours floated by, he thought of his mother, her tallness, her military posture, the black clothes she had always been stuffed into. In marrying her husband she declared she'd married a bucket. Her face looked a bit like a bucket itself.

Bert had recovered his poise. The width of his shoulders breathed again. His chest was out. It was that evening a young man wearing a scarlet tie stopped and talked to him under a particularly dusky tree by Hyde Park. 'You're Irish,' the young man had said. 'How do you know?' 'Those sparkling blue eyes.' The young man had worn a kind of perfume himself. 'You know,' he said – his accent was very posh – 'There's going to be a war. You would be better off in Ireland.' Bert considered the information. 'I'm here on a course.' Between that remark and a London hotel there was an island of nothing. Masculine things for Bert had always been brothers pissing, the spray and the smell of their piss, smelly Protestants in the cricket changing rooms. That night Bert – how he became one he did not know – was a body. His youth was in the hands of an Englishman from Devon. The creaminess of his skin and the red curls of his hair had attained a new state for one night, that of an angel at the side of the Gothic steeple at home. There was beauty in Bert's chest. His penis was in the fist of another young man.

Marriage, children, a drapery business in Ireland virtually eliminated it all but they could not quite eliminate the choice colours of sin, red of handkerchiefs in men's pockets in a smoky hotel lounge, red of claret wine, red of blood on sheets where love-making was too violent. In the morning there was a single thread of a red hair on a pillow autographed in pink.

When my father opened his drapery business he ran it by himself for a while but on his marriage he felt the need for an assistant and Patsy was the first person who presented himself for the job. It was Patsy's black hair, his child's lips, his Roman sky-blue eyes that struck a resonance in my father. Patsy came on an autumn day. My father was reminded of a night in London. His partnership with Patsy was a marital one. When I came along it was me over my brothers Patsy chose. He was passing on a night in London. The young man in London? He'd worn a scarlet tie. My father specialized in ties. Patsy wore blue and emerald ones to town dos. He was photographed for the

Connaught Tribune in a broad, blue, black speckled one. His shy smile hung over the tie. Long years ago my mother knew there was something missing from her marriage to my father – all the earnest hot water jars in the world could not obliterate this knowledge. She was snidely suspicious of Patsy – she too had blackberry hair – and when Patsy's denouement came along it was she who expelled him from the shop, afraid for the part of her husband he had taken, afraid for the parcel of her child's emotions he would abduct now that adolescence was near. But the damage, the violation had been done. Patsy had twined my neck in a scarlet tie one sunny autumn afternoon in the shop, tied it decorously and smudged a patient, fat, wet kiss on my lips.

Grief

By complete chance they arrived in the town with a party from Dublin who swarmed about the town in their capacity as members of a mystery tour. Fleshy Dublin working-class mothers suddenly realized the folly of having come on the mystery tour and this realization was evident. The sun made feeble efforts to grimace through clouds and many of the fleshy women were bravely bedecked in summer blouses. The odd child had a balloon dangling over his or her head and some children carried buckets and spades, having been certain it seemed that the mystery tour would take them to a shore. There was no shore here apart from a sliver of beach at one side of the river. But the mystery tour members would have a job finding that. They drifted, with determination in their eyes, the mile or so into town and to the desultory icecream parlours and fish and chip shops and to the one sit-down restaurant where, in the words of the knowing, maggoty portions of chicken were served. The mystery tour was a delectation of Dubliners. You booked on it, not knowing what part of Ireland it would take you to. All mystery tours were done by train. Why the minds behind it should choose this town few people could ever guess, but the irony of it today was that all the people on the mystery tour were coming as participants in a backdrop to Lettuce's and Nacker's first voyage home in decades.

Sanity came and went with them like the sun on this day: sometimes during the train journey, Lettuce, under her scarf, would make very coherent conversation. Other times she'd become agitated and eventually almost start winnowing, like some frail object caught in a strong breeze. But there was orchestration, rhythm, even language in her winnowing which had been an actual habit of hers for years.

To most of the Dubliners on the train they were probably an eccentric country pair. But their story went much further than that and this journey was more spectacular than that.

Nacker was a young soldier in the new Free State army. The new army had commandeered the Railway Hotel, a terracotta, large Swiss-chalet-type building on a hillock beside the station, for headquarters. Nacker could often be seen outside it, in summer; shirt off, polishing his gun. He was handsome. His body had a tortuous muscularity. He was of the tinkers. Thus the name Nacker. But his comrades called him Knickers because of the long strawberry underpants they saw him wear and because of his reputation with the ladies. Lettuce was one of these ladies. She was Lettie then.

The town after the civil war seemed to exhale life, the spindly, admonitory spire of the Catholic church. Girls like Lettie pulled up their skirts by the river with sacramental candour as they trod the low-depth stretches of the river which had the Well of the Nun to the other side of them. The Well of the Nun was a holy well called after a medieval, local nun who dispensed many miracles but had been tricked out of sainthood by jealous males. Girls like Lettie rejoiced in the intoxicating expectation of the aftermath of a revolution, forgetting that they were also living in the aftermath of a civil war in which many local jugular veins had been slashed. There had been a briefly lived sexual liberation in the mid 1920s – not unlike the sportive liberation of boys on school outing.

Lettie had been a maiden of the revolution. She had a white dress on when Nacker first saw her, in the river. Her hair was a pagan, evenly brushed out abundance over her olive skin. She had been transported from a land of black grapes and white dresses at the high point of the revolution. In fact it was just Lettie Loughnane who had grown up and Nacker, if he stretched his mind, would have realized he'd seen her many times before, a lizard-like schoolgirl from the slums of town, the street called after that enthusiast for the Irish working classes, Queen Victoria. Nacker was from an outlying string of new houses, too sparse to be a slum, but also accommodating the poor and the deranged. Nettle Row it was nicknamed. Nacker's mother had a forest of nettles growing outside her house and could often be seen to look out at this forest as if it was her prize in life.

Nacker looked at Lettie with bravura and was determined to seduce her. He did, after the St John's Eve Fair. His body was a heavy mantle of nakedness over her, that seemed to fall into the little secretive beads of midsummer grass, the midsummer harvest of long grass.

Now Nacker had a flaw. He was violent. And when he killed another soldier in a brawl he was ordered by a judge, who decided he was mad, into the local mental hospital. The local mental hospital in the 1920s was no place for a sensually charged young man who wore demon red underpants, that had been sent, swathed in brown paper, from London. There Nacker, with the chemicals given to him, with the treatment of freezing baths and purges of the bowels, did become undeniably mad. The killing of the soldier in the brawl had been accidental. A Titan clout in the chin. But what was done to Nacker Cluskey by the town was totally deliberate and almost self-consciously cold-blooded. For his most sensual, his most physical years he was locked away, and passing schoolgirls, in dolorous and profuse navy, were surprised to see behind iron bars a Rudolph Valentino-looking mad man with an unquenched lava of desire in his eyes.

Lettie too came to watch those eyes, outside the mental hospital window, and it was said that it was in this way she became mad, a duet of madness going between her and Nacker. She too ended up in the mental hospital, in a different part from Nacker, but at least she could see him occasionally, both of them walking round in circles in the same yard on Sundays, she in the female circle, he in the male. One day they eloped to England. That was in the late 1930s. They were already somewhat middle-aged. The story was that an admiring female relative gave them the money, the clothes, the baggage: a relative who admired their relationship. Lettie or Lettuce as she was known now escaped from Ireland in a fawn, lizard-like coat, with a scarf on her head, a white scarf with patterns of foliage on it which could have been lettuce.

What brought them back decades later? Memory, an exasperating turbulence of mutual memory culminating in a memory of the holy well, the place of the woman, the healing water and the healing, adjoining, foot-smoothed stone. After decades of wandering around England as tramps, as bizarre Irish people, they both needed to be healed or at least return to the country which had assassinated their hold on sanity. They needed a dignity of Irish nation before dying. Only the well, the well in memory, could give them that.

Past Kilrehill's English-postbox-red shop with packets of cornflakes arranged in the window by Mrs Kilrehill, since 1946 it seemed, two rows of them, the illustrations of cornflakes on the boxes gone the colour of hay in January light, the illustrations about to fade from existence altogether: beneath this blatant manifestation of favouritism for cornflakes, a few prostrate packets of washing powder on a slanted part of the base of the window, just next to the glass. Inside the shop all sorts of curious, almost cabbalistic jars of outmoded sweets. The finicky figure of Mrs Kilrehill in the dusk of the shop. The smell of the 1930s coming out, or at least of a long bygone decade, reassuring Lettuce and Nacker. The mausoleum smell in their nostrils as they passed the beginning of the convent precinct which bordered on the street.

Far behind these buildings once, in a convent meadow evenly patterned with cypress trees, Sister Honoria sat beside her aviary. Sister Honoria, aged at least a hundred, the lime and lemon and vermilion birds talking to one another behind her and she talking to herself, the colours mixing in her monologue, the anecdotes, the parts of history, the birds squawking, her birds, collected over the years, the species breeding and ongoing, and her monologue becoming fiercer and louder as she came to a particularly ravaged part of history, then quiet coming, evening descending, a yellow ochre benediction over the convent meadow, with its cypress trees, beside a river which curved to the distant mental hospital buildings, only a silent nun left, who, exhausted of monologue, seemed to personify the trance of evening peace, a smile on her like a downward crack on a yellow teapot. Sister Honoria gave Lettuce a picture of the Little Flower of Lisieux once and told her always to keep her heart pure, like the Little Flower, the old nun pressing Lettuce's hand with a grasp light and ethereal as manna from Heaven, a final little tightening in the grasp meant to convince.

Lettuce forged onwards, back slanted. She and Nacker passed the part of the convent with a porch in which, if you went in, you could see, through glass, the theatricals of Our Lady of Lourdes appearing to Bernadette. This happening was kept in semi-darkness, like a show for lewd old men. Lettuce and Nacker did not wish to see it. Even after years the stripe of blue of Our Lady's sash was indented in their minds.

But other things were prominent in what was almost their mutual consciousness now. They both looked down and you knew they were tormented. There was a hastening, determined energy in their movements. But despite this determination and sense of purpose, pain and desolation showed through. Eyes on the limestone pavement they were reminded of what the limestone pavements of this town had brought them to. In fact the sights of memory were given a fresh and searing – searing as gull's wings in the winter sunlight of Northumberland – illumination with their return.

The doss-houses of England, the dung heaps of humanity in them, the smell of dung, of damp coats, of mouldering facial hair, the zany smiles, the dazed eyes: most participants in this ritual Irish. Sanity and sense knocked way back in the whites of eyes. Stories here, rejections. Madness, hallucination, even an idiotic merriment left. Lettuce and Nacker went from one doss house to another. They knew the North of England best, towns of disused mills and hummocks of hills. They were a legend. The doss houses they stayed in were the tags on their existence. They made a pattern of these tags, albeit a frenetic pattern as they quickly went from one to another to prove something. Somehow they felt most at home in Yorkshire. Yorkshire reminded them of Ireland. The accent, and the ocean of dun in the moors, the psychic, primeval tidings that seemed to blow in from these moors, connecting all primeval, haunted places.

Where they came from with its workhouse and mental hospital was a primeval place.

Now they were on the Elysian grandeur of Thobias Street – Toby Street for short – not all that much changed, the Presbyterian church still there, the doleful Presbyterian church that collected a few worshippers on Sundays, who pulled up outside it in the town's first motor cars. The Presbyterian church beside the Horticultural Society. Fruit cakes awarded prizes there each year by the local landlord. The top winner of a fruit cake crowned with a tiara that was supposed to have sat on a music-hall comedienne's head in London. The Horticultural Society now the sit-down restaurant. Members of the mystery tour had already found their way there and were being given plates in a worried kind of way by anaemic waitresses. In a drapery shop window a torso wore scarlet underpants.

'O Nacker, do it to me until I'm sore with you.' On a midsummer night once there had been individual rainbows over big stems of grass. The two of them had repeated the act of love over England. First time they'd made love after the years in the mental hospital was in a hotel in Dublin. The Lord Lieutenant Hotel. A wilting Georgian building full of statues of Mary and of skeletal-throated washbasins. In a grotto of a room where damp covers were piled on the bed and a Fenian leader conspired on the wall, his portrait there among the colonial, ancient browns. Making love brought back sanity. For a night and a morning. The morning after they had tapering glasses of vanilla ice cream, running with red and with pastoral green, in O'Connell Street. After that there was a boat on a damp day.

To remember the first act of love was to remember sanity. Going down the street they almost remembered. The integrity of his body. The lack of experience of hers. As first-time lovers, remembering that, they'd rediscover sanity. That's why they'd come home. To know first sensuality again. That memory, which they knew to be always there but which defied their reach, was the custodian of their sanity and their integrity as human beings. That's where they were heading now. To the mirror of the well to identify – with the help of the well's benefactress, the nun, the lady – their lost totality.

Sometimes along the way, on their journeys, they saw young men and young women who reminded them. A young man on a beach in Northumberland in the 1950s, scarlet swimming togs on him, his body held up, almost hypnotized into silence, against an unfolding of an aeroplane trail in the sky behind him, a trail which could have been an embroidery in the County Galway summer sky in the 1920s. A young soldier outside a barracks in the 1960s. His hair both blond and brown. Again, something hypnotized about his stance. As if he was suddenly fixated by a message between different decades. His face under that blond and brown hair still almost a child's, all rabbit-white. Tremulous. Dancers beside a beach, rock and roll dancers, a boy and a girl, on a summer evening, on a platform, jiving away, the lights of a spectacular promontory at one side of the beach dipping into the sea, tendrils of light connecting with promenade-side tendrils of fish and chip shop and amusement arcade lights. Then there'd been a little boy near the Scottish border who'd held his hands behind his back and stared at them, his hair chestnut-coloured, freckles falling like bits of turf beneath his eyes, something entranced about his eyes as if he could remember days in autumn when Nacker sat outside the Free State army headquarters as children passed him, heading back to the bogs beyond the railway station, one bog indeterminate from another in their flushes of purple and mauve, Nacker's thoughts, then, on Lettuce but melancholic, foreboding, autumnal thoughts. He knew, even then, after their first summer, as he bit tobacco, that something would be destroyed in him. He knew at nights that autumn as he sent billiard balls wailing into their sockets. He knew as his figure, standing, addressed the cinema screen. Yes, I am almost back there he thought now. Almost back there. He had almost returned to that threshold when he was still sane but he knew something was about to give, not so much in him, as in fate.

A bullet whirred through the Blackwoods that winter. An old, otter-like lady in a black coat pushed a pram, looking for firewood. Nacker walked the Blackwoods that winter, incessantly, trying to escape his fate. The colours of the horizons, mangled firework effects, were the colours of his mind.

Philosophy there and treatises on life. Symphonies too. Once he'd heard Beethoven's *Eroica* Symphony coming from a gramophone in the local landlord's house and that had stayed in his mind. It played in his mind the first day he was put into the mental hospital.

Down by the market square they were now. Lettuce had once danced here to mark in the new year. Fishy Shanahan, the keeper of the canal lock house, alternatively called Captain Shanahan, had played his melodion. Someone had lit a bonfire and a contrary woman opened her cottage door which adjoined the square and bellowed at them that they should all be making penitence in their beds. 'Yea, soiling the sheets with their salaciousness,' someone had shouted. What Lettuce and Nacker could not know now was that Fishy Shanahan had recently died, his body brought up the steel stairway outside his house by the square, his wife waiting for the body on the top. He'd fallen in the square. 'Fishy,' she'd cried, 'Fishy'. Red coming to her cheeks like an attestation of healthiness. He'd been called Fishy partly because of her. She was the market fish seller. And partly, of course, he'd been called Fishy because he was the keeper of the canal lock house. Then again there was another reason. Because people had thought he was a bit fishy ever since they'd never really known what side he'd identified with during the civil war. Grief. This town was full of grief. Lettuce and Nacker could not have known about Fishy's recent death in the square and the pageant of his body being carried up the steel stairway to his waiting wife but being ascribed mad they could feel the freshness of its reverberations. They could feel all the recent grief.

Turgid in stance they walked by the river. On the other side now men with greyhounds were going hunting hares. Among them Ambrose Kelly, illegitimate son of an Italian woman who'd found an Irish name for herself somewhere along the way. She'd lived over Croffey's pub until her death a few years previously, a death as desultory as her life. She'd lived over Croffey's pub around which Guinness barrels were arranged all over the place like ammunition, singing Italian arias, taking male clients to her bed; Ambrose, when he was a child, watching this, from over a table, raspberry jam on his face. His mother had reared him on raspberry jam, doses of it, because that had seemed to stultify his crying. The bits of raspberry flesh had clung to his face like a disease. He'd been a silent child, never speaking much; then when he'd been fifteen he'd fallen down the hole for further supplies of alcohol, outside the pub, and permanently injured his left leg. He'd limped ever since, had been awarded compensation from which he still eked out a living, plastering his face over the same table with tomato sauce from pasta rather than with raspberry jam. At nineteen he'd begun to sing himself. Arias from Italian operas. He performed in Croffey's bar each Sunday morning, the Croffey being the people he and his mother had brought to court because of the accident. But all was amiably settled now. A bad leg for him. Songs for them. His favourite *'Che Gelida Manina'* from *La Bohème*. People came from all over to listen. They knew he'd inherited his mother's habit of picking up strangers. Though little was spoken of that. In his case it was boys. Last night he'd had a boy from Dublin. A dazed-looking young man in his early twenties who'd been wandering down Thobias Street late at night with a famished-looking haversack thrown on his back. They'd made love silently and then the boy had gone this morning. Then there were arias in the pub. Now hare hunting. At twenty-two Ambrose Kelly had lost his hair. He was now parallel to Lettuce and Nacker. And just as he was parallel, without seeing them, he began singing for some reason *'Che Gelida Manina'*. Lettuce and Nacker looked up, not over. They were near the holy well.

Love and desire; last night love in a grotty room where the pasta had not been cleaned from the saucepans; years ago love in the grass at midsummer. Two odysseys of love merging now; one brief, lasting a night, the other lasting years. The young Dublin man had given his name as Adolphe. That was obviously a lie. He'd gone on to Galway on the train which had brought the mystery tour from his native Dublin to the town.

What was it that made a human being destroy love and equilibrium? What exploded Nacker into a temper the night of the brawl in the Free State army headquarters? A young man of handsomeness, intelligence and earnest curiosity, why had he left a life of hope behind with an animalistic brawl in which he killed someone? Who knows? Perhaps he'd seen that a life of radical integrity, of continuing passion could not have gone on. Perhaps the fight had come from an irrational, untamed part of him which was not known to the other part. But the irrational, untamed part had killed the potential of the earnest young man. They had become confused, they had become entwined in a brawl of their own and Nacker's potential was laid out for life. Or was it? Had something survived?

Nacker could see himself as a young man now, sensuality qualifying sensuality on him. And the woman who'd followed him to madness? She was beside him. Yes they had proved something. They had lived their life as an act and at the end of their life come to the holy well to shed the act, the mask; but would the mask come off?

They were now passing the part of the river where a ginger-haired young man had been found drowned the week just gone, a bag beside him in the river containing three ginger cocker spaniels, stones in it too. No one had known where he or they had come from.

A voice kept going in Lettuce's head. Or was it Lettie's head? 'You'll spend all your life pretending, Lettie Loughnane.' It was a nun's voice. A nun from school. The sun had come out and they were beside the well. Two figures stood, dismantled of, embarrassed out of insanity, by a well which was not a holy well or a nun's well or the well of the woman – the woman had gone – but a trap for water with the carcass of a very heavy television thrown into it. A television that must have been very heavy to carry here for such a malign and rancorous-smelling burial spot. A bit of paper stirred inside the broken frame of the television, a picture of a young Irish pop star on it, the pop star in a Valentine pink suit and he smiling a message at Lettuce and Nacker.

They spent that summer, a very hot summer, living in a doss house in Brighton, the sight of Nacker with his shirt off, showing his aged bone cage, becoming familiar on the beach, the man standing as though hypnotized by something and no sign of Lettuce who was lost among the tulip-beds of sun-bathing women, an image connecting their minds though, one that had occurred to Lettuce first at the well, that of the cinema in the town in the 1920s with its coffin-like smells and those jittery, ever-beckoning images on the screen, images of Arabs and of sailors. They had followed those images, completing the circle, back to a bit of water which was the well on a Sunday when clouds and sun raced across that dark and dour and ever-imbued County Galway greenery.

'Lettie,' Nacker called to Lettuce that summer as she sunbathed on a beach. She looked up to see a man in a hallucination of sun who might have been a young man, his shirt off, a cravat of kind of Punch and Judy patterns, large strawberries of red on yellowy white, around his naked neck. And on the beach in Brighton she saw a Punch and Judy show, replete with loud noises and rude explosions, being performed against the Victorian workhouse at home, as she died; a young, very muscle-conscious, hot sand-bleached life guard, in scarlet swimming togs, bending over the gnarled and rickety old woman to give her, out of some whim, the kiss of life.

The Vicar's Wife

1

1959 was the year Joly won the local beauty competition and the year Colin came down from Trinity as a teddyboy vicar, a bouncing limousine of black hair in front of his forehead. 1959 was the year in which everything dangled precipitously on a scales, past and future, the end of things, the initiation of other things. There was something fearful about the things beginning. It was the year Joly and Colin met and became lovers.

There was such a mind-boggling difference in their backgrounds that their pairing didn't so much cause anger as a kind of earthquake; Barna Craugh's earthquake, 1959, the narrow roadway of Bin Lane opened and devoured a lady or two who had to walk up this disreputable lane because it connected the church with their part of town. Off Bin Lane Joly had been born. 'Born brown-haired!' people pronounced over and over again. Because now her award-winning curls were a cheeky peroxide blonde. It was her tits that had got her the prize, uncouth and bellicose farm labourers insisted. Her breasts were very large and she didn't try to sunder their largeness. It was those breasts the vicious and the jealous swore to themselves had attracted the attention of Vicar Colin Lysaght. Although much of the ultimate version was that he'd picked up a Catholic rose and transformed her into a black Protestant nettle. Joly Ward converted to Protestantism to marry the teddyboy vicar.

The house was the most immeasurable leap for her; the house she moved into. It changed her automatically, from beauty queen to dark-haired, demure Protestant wife. Fear. That was the first word that came to her in the house. Fear filled her to a point at which she thought she was going to explode with it. But she kept silent. Shadows wrapped around her, twisted around her, shadows of dark banisters. Joly was in a house in the country, suffocated by gardens and by trees.

The wedding had been a pantomime, a joke, mainly lizard-like, old eccentric vicars at it, a flotsam of young ex-Trinity-students. Ascendancy heirs rushed at champagne glasses, young men in snappily white shirts and in dark, casually askew jackets. There was a quick snow of champagne on a number of young, nearly-black moustaches. Joly was a proof of a Protestant sense of humour, a testimony to Irish eccentric Protestantism's ability to laugh at itself. She was in the line of a tradition of jokes; that day a dummy in white, an unwitting foible. Young ascendancy men gauged her breasts in her wedding dress with their eyes. But her own family didn't look at her. They, to a man, did not come to the wedding. There was no Catholic there.

If she thought of it afterwards there were mainly men there and what women were there seemed to be stuffed into ragdoll textures of garments; their faces when you went close were blanks, their eyes didn't look at you. They looked through you. They were the faces of the dead.

Dead. There was death in this house. A subtle, omnipresent whine. She remembered the Catholic churches' teachings about purgatory but this house had more the reverberations of hell. No possible escape within the mood of the house. Both Colin's parents were dead, Colin's father himself having been a vicar. She touched a banister on her first arrival as Colin's wife – Colin hadn't let her see the house up to then – clinging to it for a moment, in a blue, matronly dress, for life. She knew that moment she had lost all worlds, the world of home, and the world of frivolous, combative youth.

Joly had gone against the grain from the time she was a little girl. Decked out in her holy communion costume, a veritable fountain of a veil, Joly had stampeded towards an obese member of the local town council, a very respectable man, his collar open, and plied him – successfully – for a russet money bill. She developed a relationship with this man, himself unmarried. At public functions, a St Patrick's Day parade, the crowning of the king of the fair, she always managed to get money out of him, a little prostrate flag of hair on the otherwise bald top of his head. It was unheard of, a relationship between a member of the town council and a child from Bin Lane. As a member of the town council you could be beneficiary for the sons and daughers of army colonels, of shopkeepers, of police superintendents. But not for a child from Bin Lane. Children from Bin Lane might as well have been squirrels with a contagious disease to the respectable people of town, and tawdry, unkempt squirrels at that. You could approach them, cautiously, at Christmas, with presents, in your annual symbol of generalized support for the Vincent de Paul.

A man on the local council and Joly; a photograph in the local press. Without a jacket, the man in a white shirt, his face round like a balloon, a meteor of a smile on his face, apple flushes on his cheeks. He looked quixotically retarded. It was this photograph which was the marked beginning of Joly's break with her own world and of her steep rise to stardom, notoriety and to the social grazing area of old, beak-nosed parsons. It had been a passport for her, her countenance in the photograph full of knowingness.

In 1959 she won the local beauty competition. The events which went into this success were manifold. Joly had won a scholarship to the convent secondary school, the first girl from Bin Lane to have done so. But the nuns at convent school immediately rejected her. She smelt, despite 'her brains' as they put it, raw. They had to admit the 'brains'. Joly seemed to be able to wriggle her way around any problem and she was able to come out with all sorts of information, adding even to the nuns' store of general knowledge. But she made them baulk. She was shameless in her gait. And it was this shamelessness combined with her nearly always manifest mental ability which made her such a special beauty queen for Barna Craugh. Her hair dyed blonde she'd turned down a secretarial job with a 'top-notch' firm of solicitors in Dublin, to participate in the contest. It was both a joke and gamble for her. A joke within the vocabulary of the effervescent way she looked at life – all rampant blonde curls and daring scarlet lips – and yet an ironic intellectual thumb in every joke. Was anything worth it really? The job in Dublin she turned down to parade herself in a beauty contest. It riled her family, her decision, almost caused a revolution among them. They thought they had one member so near to success! And if it was a gamble for her it more than paid off. It seemed to bring her much further than any job with a solicitor in Dublin – after a brief secretarial course – could have done. It landed her in an altogether different stratum of society. She felt like Judy Garland when *The Wizard of Oz* turned from black and white into technicolour. Her hair turned back to brown at the same moment and all her features, as well as her converted soul, seemed to become demure and tentative and Protestant. She merged perfectly with the landscape of the rural, grey, elongated house.

There was more to Joly's sudden fame in 1959 than the winning of the beauty contest. Winning the beauty contest would not, in fact, have been spectacular in itself. Given her unusual personality as well as her sharply striking looks she got a series of national offers after winning the contest. Her face was in a ladies' magazine, advertising the luscious red lipstick she liked so much. In another advertisement her blonde curls sported a hat which looked like a pink sandcastle. She was a bride in the most widely admired advertisement photograph. And that was appropriate enough. For Colin Lysaght saw the photograph and it was as if he picked the bride from the image as he would a bit of resplendent apple blossom. They were married in May 1960. Joly, though not in any way having been persuaded to, renounced Catholicism and became a Protestant to marry the delectable youth of a vicar and be an acceptable vicar's wife.

The morning she married, the nuns in her former school had the girls there send up shoals of prayers for her soul as if she had been their penultimately prize pupil, now having made a staggering fall.

Colin had been living in a town house beside the railway station since his father's death. After the wedding he brought Joly to the rural vicarage which had been industriously painted for weeks. It had been a secret. Now the secret unfolded.

There was death and an ancient stagnation in the teddyboy vicar.

What had she really known about him? Very little. She looked at gravestones in a nearby field the following autumn. Ignat Lysaght. An ancestor of Colin's. She was pregnant with a Protestant child. She was carrying the continuity of a contorted history inside her.

Autumn was the greatest wonder in this house; the greatest torrent of technicolour in the house, apple on apple creeping across the lawn and gardens, all different in colour, some a hue of luminous gold, others more scarlet, more vermilion, apples very often a garish and unexpected clown's-cheek rouge. A gold too went into the green of the lawn, the gardens and the surrounding countryside, all of which had been a very dark and peculiar green throughout the summer. Tinkers' caravans in the backlanes had nestled in this green, taken a silent refuge among the green. Very few tinkers seemed to emerge from the caravans and if they did they were archaic faces, very often male faces, that met you silently and seemed stranded on the roadway. All was atavistic here, skeletons were suggested very close to the surface in graveyards and frequently there were bones to be seen on graves, tussled among the clay. They would be strange sights for a child.

All summer long Joly had got to know her husband and herself better.

She'd looked in a mirror and had been amazed at the physical change in herself. She'd got plumper, more demure; her eyes seemed haunted by aspects of this house and of her husband's behaviour. She'd been made to seem meek in her demeanour by what she'd come to realize. Her husband, for all his teddyboy looks, was one of the sequence of shapes of an ogre from the deepest past. He'd been contaminated and made violent by the past. That summer, before she became pregnant, he began to beat her up and the beatings continued after she discovered she was pregnant. She was in a prison. She could not go back. She had to stay where she was, with, for the moment, just one other cell-mate.

Colin's face had changed once he'd got into the house; from a protruding frigate of an adolescent face it became debauched in appearance, mean, curdled. The lips, especially, looked dehydrated. With this life-despising change came the news of new life. News of new life came, it later seemed, with a solitary visit by Joly to a dark church with one, Technicolored, stained-glass window.

But, despite change in Colin, the church she'd been received into was still a statement for her; it was a statement of surrender of old values, the values of a totalitarian premiss on life, and the choosing of something new; something more liberated, something that gave her many choices; she was a Protestant by choice, a keeper of sentinel rows of geraniums, luminous in the mellifluous, vicarage, autumn sun.

She wore black a lot at Christmas. By then she'd accepted Colin's change of personality. The funny thing was that in the atmosphere of this house, in entry into this house, she was not surprised by the change in Colin. The source was a mystery to her, the emanation of this house. She was fighting with it. She served sherries to dried, old, outstretched, Protestant fingers that Christmas.

The baby was born in April. A boy. He came with medieval-Annunciation-painting trees of apple blossom, little celebratory bolls of apple blossom. She gave birth to the child in Barna Craugh's one hospital, a Catholic hospital, and a nun, in white, eyed her threateningly, her eyes saying that for this child's sake, if not for your own, pull back from the abyss. Audoen was baptized a Protestant child in a ceremony by a rural font. A wash of pale, hallucinatory, May light came through the Technicolored window. Colin's face was alarmingly drained that day. He'd been ranting to himself in the nights previously. Another vicar, called into this parish especially, performed the ceremony.

Colin, in these days, had given himself over to Joly, asking for compassion, saying he was ill, that he had a disease, that his own father had treated his mother appallingly, that violence was rampant in male members of his family, that it was a rancid gene in the family. He was a boy in her arms now at night, the little boy who'd been cradled by other boys in a posh,

Protestant school in Dublin, the little boy who'd dreamt of the Dublin Horse Show at night among evangelically laundered sheets.

In May 1966, when Audoen was five years old, he was run over on the road near the vicarage and killed. By then Joly had two more children. Colin was no longer a teddyboy. There was a decrepit grey on the edges of his hair. For the funeral another vicar did not have to be brought in. It took place in Barna Craugh which was part of another diocese, though close to the rural one where Colin presided. Audoen was buried in the Protestant part of Barna Craugh cemetery. Colin, face anaemic and blanched, bawled at the funeral. The faces of the women of Barna Craugh peered out from a dusk of their own in the cemetery. Justice had been done. God had punished this woman. But by then the teachings of the Ecumenical Council were creeping through and there wasn't as much gloating about the event as there might have been. Joly's marriage, bound together by children and a stoic compassion, was breaking up. The only thing that held it now was wonder on Joly's part at Colin's personality, wonder as to how such violence as she'd known and continued to experience could have insinuated itself so readily into a frame as aesthetically pleasing and as, almost shockingly, susceptible to the senses as Colin's had been. He'd had a pale adolescent face you could almost eat. But that face, the good looks, had been a mask.

The little rural hell was seven years old when she left Colin. On the day she got a taxi to the station from the centre of Barna Craugh she heard someone sing a refrain from 'O Lady of Spain I adore you' on the main street. Her two children went with her. Colin had beaten her senseless with the leg of a chair a few nights previously, a leg from a chair which, before attacking her, he'd attacked, thus extracting the leg. She had bruises all over her on the main street the day she left. A woman looked closely at her, almost sympathetically. The bruises on Joly's face were like the marks of napalm. The bruises on her psyche from the vicar and from the town were worse and more enduring, as she was to find, than any television-screen napalm could suggest.

2

Comely Bank Grove, Edinburgh, was the address which she moved into with Midge, the Polish truck driver. She'd previously been living with a friend, from her school days, in Dundee. The friend had emigrated halfway through convent secondary education and the two girls had kept in touch. Joly's friend had not married, not wanted to marry. She nursed Joly, with a sense of vocation, for five years. There was a speechless communication between them, a distance, but sometimes in that distance bolts of desire from Joly's friend. But silent and ultimately stagnant bolts. The woman was so beholden to Joly for company, for purpose in life, that she even looked after Joly's children when Joly began going out with Midge. By then Barna Craugh was far away. Joly was a tart again, raspberry lipstick on her and her hair curled now, looking black rather than brown. Their most exotic occasions, hers and Midge's, were Chinese meals on Saturday nights in a Chinese restaurant among an industrial estate by the sea. Joly picked up bits of a Polish accent which she interspersed with her new Scottish accent.

Her children were Finn and Bríd. When eventually she moved in with Midge they might as well have been his children, judging by the ease of their appearance with him as they all sat around a table, joined in a meal. There was a conspiracy of pretences. But they all knew they were followed, by the sense of the children's father, by the inchoate hurt of Joly's friend. When she departed nothing in her mind had prepared her for Joly's departure. She even thought that by making it easy for Joly to see Midge she'd further strengthen her bond with Joly. But Joly went when Midge bought a house for a cheap price and there was a cocoon for her, her children, her relationship with Midge and her own confusion about herself and her past.

Not a day went by when she didn't try to unravel her relationship with Joly Ward, the multiple Joly Wards, the woman who had broken so many hearts and left so much patternless debris.

Ireland in Midge's mind was the country of grandiose scenery which they'd both seen in *Ryan's Daughter* in Dundee and Joly did not wish to disillusion him. For him she was haunted by the lofty tourist-brochure scenery which had something unexpectedly malevolent stuck in it. He did not realize and she never informed him that she came from flat land, nothing like the scenery of *Ryan's Daughter*. To have betrayed this would have been to betray a secret. You always had to keep secrets from lovers. However safe you felt with them you were also, always, on the run and you couldn't give too much away. In fact, even in love, you had to invent a pose rather than give your real self away. This was how Joly felt with Midge. Happy but incomplete. At worst an over made-up character in a pantomime. A rather idiotic character, lots of lipstick on, her neck moving around in a kitchen, to the rhythm of a conversation, like a gander's neck, a half-wit's smile on her face.

The black, almost funereal doors of Edinburgh; mystery. Joly walked alone on winter nights when rain beat on these doors. She paused in front of these doors, staring at them in a nebulous gesture. What did they remind her of? Of the door of a vicarage, painted gleaming black. Of a brass knocker with a Cupid at its nub. Of a demure, dignified vicar's wife. Of the choice of hers to love a strange man. Colin. She was still under the spell of love for him. There was still a romantic yearning in her for a young cleric in black, with a teddyboy flop of hair on front of his forehead; there was still a belief in her that the purity of this young man still existed. It only had to come to the surface, through complex effort and through earnest search. The past, the black bits of it, could be dispelled. The black bits in Colin came from a general blindspot in his ancestry. He only had to go through it, walk through it to the other side. Easier said than done. But everything was possible. She knew then he was searching for her. She wondered would he catch up on her. There were two persons in her now, the person who wanted him to find her and the tart who, partly out of laziness, wished to be without him. These parts of her were at war.

There was a war going on in Ireland. The rain here waged a war in sympathy to the mood of the war in Ireland. People rebuffed Joly for this war, mainly women. Irish. Irish had a dirty ring these days. Bodies. Mutilations. The bomb that surprised you from under your restaurant seat. Joly had to undergo the ritual of demoralization, because of the race she was from, again and again. Made to do so by people who understood nothing of Ireland or nothing of history. The incessancy of this eventually caused the straight beauty queen figure to look pinched, to have a hint of middle age in it.

The year Joly came to look middle-aged she went South with Midge in his truck, on one of his journeys, through Yugoslavia to Greece and back.

The oxen in the fields, the peasant women, the rain of sun on the readiness of corn; renewal. Marigolds in a vase in a café in Belgrade, o so lucid white wine in carafes on the shelf. Outside a man sweeping up a searing dash of yellow ochre leaves. The smell from those leaves; what did it remind her of? A vicarage. The first time she'd ever really experienced autumn.

She'd been a gauche girl before knowing autumn, but autumn, the smell of the leaves, of the opaque-gold apples, of the rain-haggard dwarf dahlias opened her to many other things; a view of life that transcended anything she'd known before. Autumn, a vicarage in the autumn, was history. It was a symbol of the subjugation of the land she came from. Remorse in some people who'd subjugated that land turned to terror, terror on wife, son, terror on self. Colin's father had committed suicide.

That floret of information was kept to the very end; squeezed tight in Colin's pale hands all those years. Colin's father had beaten him, tried to debilitate him in every way. The young man she'd encountered, who'd just come down from Trinity, was a temporarily escaped version of Colin, Colin after a few years of exuberance and oblivion. But there was the Colin tied to family. The demon Colin. History, family history, had not been worked through in Colin. And he took this inability to cope with what his father had tried to do with him out on Joly. In a kind of loyalty to his father he was crazed with his wife. There was a kind of metamorphosis that occurred late in the Lysaght night. Not only the suicide of Colin's father was lived over and over again in Colin but the vicious instincts which led to the suicide.

Something was alive in Colin. A family ogre, a bogey man, untrammelled evil itself. Joly was to have been the cure for the evil, her peroxide curls were the bait, but she too became a victim to the evil. She left. But there was something she'd done. She'd set an erratic process of redemption in motion in Colin. She'd initiated a humility in his eyes. They were eyes she nearly saw telepathically in moments of intensity in a kitchen in Edinburgh when the music was uncharacteristically evocative on Radio 2.

3

Colin Lysaght had had a favourite toy when he was a child. A horse, white, with a scarlet drape on it. The horse had lain in a garden behind the house, inanimate there, striking against the verdure, always reassuring in its subliminal inanimateness. This had been one of the few tokens of peace when he'd been a child. His father, Vicar Lysaght, outwardly a piece of genteel grey, his frame sometimes seeming to have been festooned in apple-tree lichen, had catatonic, totally transforming fits behind the doors and windows of the vicarage. He used to beat his wife, his son, lock his son in the nursery for hours with just a little, overfilled chamber pot for company, and a long-redundant playpen. Once Colin noticed apple blossom against a blue sky outside the nursery when he was locked in it and knew he'd escape some day.

Trinity College, Dublin; what fun. Colin was one of the brightest and the most popular of the students. Although following in his father's footsteps to be a vicar he headed some of the wildest of forays from Trinity, to the mountains, the sea, to dungeons of flats where bodies eventually twinned, in a sort of inveterate way. Colin was the rock and rolling would-be vicar, he led a dance once in a marquee, in his black clerical clothes, his oiled and extravagant hair as black. The idea of being a vicar seemed a clever extension of and a foil to being a rock and roll dancer. But still Colin passed all examinations with distinction and was ordained a vicar. He came down to Barna Craugh, just in time to meet Joly in her hour of success. The marriage was perfect, between the rock and roll vicar and the Bin Lane Marilyn Monroe. A few months before Colin was ordained a vicar though, his father had committed suicide and the impact of this event was still subsumed in rock and roll music as was the death of Colin's mother at the end of Colin's first year at Trinity. These events took their toll – after the wedding photographs.

4

Shortly after Joly left Colin gave up the trappings of being a vicar and went away himself, to Dublin, where he got a job teaching divinity and English literature in a boys' Protestant school. The black clerical clothes were exchanged for a characteristic chestnut sportscoat. The grey edges arbitrarily went from Colin's hair and it all became a subdued black, more curls in it, more divides. The vicarage had in fact belonged to the Lysaght family. So had a house in Barna Craugh. There was a complicated deal made whereby if they were sold most of the money went to the diocese where Colin and his father had functioned as vicars. Colin sold both houses. He got a small part of the price but what, for the needs of his life now, was a substantial amount of money. He banked most of that money for a secret, long-term plan. In Dublin he rented a second-floor flat in Terenure, near the school where he taught. He merged into his environment, becoming a leading member in the local branch of the Anti-Apartheid Movement, and of Amnesty International. He protested outside rugby pitches where South African teams played. He was photographed, looking distraught on these occasions, among the mêlée outside rugby pitches, by the *Irish Times*. He became a familiar protester on the front page of the *Irish Times*. Few people could have realized that this mellifluous-faced, rather autumnal-looking young man had been a wife-beater, in fact a wife-torturer. Colin shelved his secret on the neon-lit, late-1960s and early-1970s Dublin night. He bellowed protests at South Africans. He held a red flag against the sky outside the American embassy – the red was in fact part of a batik depicting Vietnamese blood, not the red of a communist flag. The October sun eddied through the batik in Ballsbridge. Flower children followed Colin, a line of Protestant, middle-class girls who had long, Pre-Raphaelite, blonde hair and who wore long, fussily floral dresses. Colin became a perfect child of his time and environment.

But he never stopped thinking of Joly and of his children: alone at night in a flat in Terenure, among the sheets soiled with haphazard, bachelor discharges, close to the socks that looked well during the day but smelt at night. In his bedroom the Dublin suburban night came in, the mountains – he kept the curtains always open – and excavated his mind. There were two Colin Lysaghts. The one he was running from. And the one he was now. But each time he imagined Joly both seemed to merge, in contrition. He knew he had to see her again. But he knew the risk of a journey to her. He had sanity in the covert-self he was now. Maybe he'd lose that sanity when he saw her. Anyway he didn't know where she was other than that she was in Scotland. He couldn't confront her family. So the years drifted until he had a letter from Joly. She wrote to say she needed to divorce him, to marry a Polish truck-driver.

5

Two people confronted in a kitchen in Edinburgh.

Colin said: 'Don't worry. I'm different.'

Joly said nothing.

Colin said: 'It's been hard. Being without you.'

Joly said nothing.

Colin said: 'The children?'

Joly said: 'They'll be in later.'

Colin said: 'Joly, I love you.'

Joly looked at him. She knew her face had become hard. She said nothing. She was the aged one. He was the younger one. There was almost a visible passage of bitterness, of sarcasm, through her face and then she knew that that wasn't worthy of this encounter and she softened. 'I'll make tea.'

She meandered almost drunkenly towards the stove. Scarlet print on a calendar told her it was August 1979.

The children came in later, Finn, Bríd, teenagers. Bríd was in emerald. Idiotically Colin thought she looked like an overgrown child in an Irish dance costume. There was no ambiguity about Finn's dress. He had metal earrings and his hair shot up in black, electric protest. Colin felt there should be a mediator, a talcum-haired priest from Ireland, a Reverend Mother from a local, prison-looking school, to negotiate them into some accord with one another; he made an erratic and abortive attempt to rise. But Finn saved the day. In heavy, working-class Scottish accent he said, 'Da, you've nearly axed yourself shaving.' Colin had badly cut his face shaving that morning.

Midge had gone. He'd left a month before. Having come to England in his early twenties he'd driven back to Poland. His mother was still in Warsaw and Warsaw, before his planned marriage in Edinburgh, got the better of him. He had to return there. He'd take it all, soldiers, police, everything for the sake of wholeness missing in his life for twenty-five years and for a kind of harvest-dream of Warsaw. He bade goodbye to Joly and the children and drove a company truck East to Warsaw, on an authorized errand, but this time he was going to stay. All that was left of Poland now were obsessive jars and jars of paprika and a picture of a Polish Christ. That picture made Colin think his wife and children were fervent Catholics now.

A working-class Edinburgh woman looked at a daintily dressed Dublin teacher. The social chasm was even wider and more perplexing than when they'd married. Colin looked like a harmless, over-trained chimpanzee now, all bones and angles. A woman, standing, looked at him, amazed at the scene that was happening. The children stared at him with convoluted stares as if they'd been expecting him all their lives and now that he'd arrived the epiphany was a curiosity more than a major event. Each time Colin opened his mouth now he shut it very quickly again, without saying anything. Joly suddenly remembered the seas of flagrant furze in the fields around the vicarage in spring.

It was her family she'd had to fight more than Colin then. They'd never imagined she'd made any really fundamental decision without consulting them, without involving them – they saw her as irritating them, driving them into furies. But when the moment came when Joly parted from them and became a Protestant they became petrified in their speech. It was unheard of, an Irish Catholic girl becoming a Protestant. An Irish Catholic girl acting on her own volition. An Irish person breaking from the rules, the taboos of their family. An Irish person going it alone, without their tribe. You could have tiffs, yes, but fleeing your family . . . May God forgive her.

Joly had shaped a solitude inside herself in a society not made for solitude. She could hear their rancour in the vicarage gardens, their screams of bellicose outrage came to her ears. But she left these things some way outside her and resolved on going further on her own way, on plunging deeper into her perdition. Perdition took her to Scotland, to Edinburgh, to a kitchen where she'd tried to lock up all the pain of Ireland and throw it away. But she couldn't help arguing with them, taking them on in a mental wrestling match during an afternoon women's programme on radio, venting her opinions of them on them. They'd done everything in their power to destroy her, to strip her of her sensibility and make her one of them. This was what was left of the battle, this still outraged shell, this shell through which visible shivers of anger often went. They'd tried to divest her of everything that was her personality, besieging her in the vicarage. Yes she knew they were out there. And perhaps that sense of siege added unsteadiness to Colin's unhinged state. The vibrations going between Joly and her family, the smoke signals of livid argument. Something of what had happened in the vicarage was Joly's fault. There was a battle pressed inside her, a battle she couldn't share with him because he was one of the main reasons for the battle. She couldn't give them any success by having him drawn into the argument. They thought, ultimately, she was less than him. She couldn't let him know she feared that also. She couldn't let their stinking

thoughts pollute her relationship with him. But in resisting
them, in keeping them at bay, in the frozen stance she adopted
any time she considered anything to do with them she off-set
something in Colin; whining choirs of his own hereditary
demons. Their mutal demons met in the vicarage and created an
abysmal furore, sometimes at the top of the stairs when, late at
night, she and Colin looked in one another's eyes. The aspect of
her blame, blame for what she'd brought to the vicarage, was
one she'd always ignored. She too had an insanity caused by
family. There had been a hole in her head, too. A transfixed void
in her eyes. Two mad people couldn't have gone on living
together and she left Colin, not without first having driven him
to beat her, to flail his arms at her. She just hadn't been capable
of response to his demons. So preoccupied and, in a way, in
love had she been with her own. She'd failed the trusting
teddyboy. She'd gone away, carrying a further retinue of self-
righteous wounds, from Ireland, edified by her own sense of
wounds. Now, the wounds had come full circle and encountered his wounds again. This time she knew she'd made the
central wound in his life. She'd failed, totally, to drive away the
dark in him. She'd been a bit of blonde mischief that had failed
to understand the trust he was putting in her. He'd totally
surrendered himself to her and all she'd done was look over his
shoulder, arguing with the spectres of her family. The arms,
legs, torso of a teddyboy vicar, naked then, had counted for
nothing, this show of tenderness, as against confrontation with
a tribe, drawn up in battle ranks by a bedroom door. Privacy had
been impossible between Colin and Joly. History and family had
not allowed them privacy. But at least they'd stolen one or two
pages from an epoch and danced together, before marriage, at
an October fair, a couple, a marriage of opposites, beauty queen
and vicar, an ikon – the ikon warmed by browns and golds,
taking a bronze light from a marquee floor, shelving an image in
a village mind, in a perpetuity of images. Together, ironically,
Colin and Joly enhanced history. They were, that night, dancing
to Buddy Holly, an atavistic reference point to which people
would always return, in spite of themselves. They were a source
of mystery, something of history and yet that broke with

history. They were initiators. What came after didn't matter so much. They'd broken new ground together and as such would always have an odd craving for one another, be in default without one another. They were, in a strange way, one.

How he could have done those things to her he didn't know. They were all a strange dream in him now. In her arms, in bed, all the people he'd been since spiralled through him, the roles. The only reality was her face and body. He touched that face and body. His hands were no longer anointed hands. They had no special powers. They were no longer cursed. They retreated from her with a sense of redemption. He looked at them in amazement, as if he was seeing them for the first time. They, he and Joly, were starting right from the beginning. No demon in his past was telling him he had to be a vicar, was entrancing him into perpetuating this role in the family. He'd shed the need for this role. Joly was no longer the vicar's wife.

7

A new term in Dublin; a new direction in Colin's thoughts, a new countenance on him. He meditated more. He slumped into meditation at school, a chestnut-coloured jacket still on him. He'd journeyed from a Protestant, middle-class, Dublin experience to a house in Edinburgh where there was a woman he'd created in a way, a strange product of Ireland. There were so many lines on her face, so many. Lines further emphasized by a cloth she'd worn on her head a few times; amid the lines an always fresh swipe of strawberry lipstick. This had been his spouse. And his children? They were more like a brother and sister to the mellifluous-looking hulk of a man who'd crossed forty with an adolescent haze still around him. He had to deal with the new image of Joly, Joly with a penetratingly direct stare in her eyes. Joly as a very lonely woman, a sentinel of a woman in the middle of a kitchen.

Colin dragged his feet around Dublin; crimson autumn suns over the Halfpenny Bridge temporarily immobilized him. The way he dragged one of his feet that autumn he looked lame. And he also looked a bit hunch-backed. He was weighed down. Weighed down by what he'd done. By the rather awesome vision of Joly standing in the middle of a kitchen, something grandiose about her, something haunting, like the way a lighthouse on the West coast of Ireland, during early-winter twilight, haunted. Joly was total unto herself. She created a sense of scenery wherever she went. And it was this loneliness that made him love her again, made him want her, maybe out of guilt, made him want to protect the wounded frame of her, reach his arms about it. So correspondence began again and, from Dublin, supplications. They wrote to one another like teenage pen-pals, from two totally different backgrounds and aware of the different backgrounds. Except now the different backgrounds were Dublin middle class and Edinburgh, downbeat working class. Joly agreed to visit Colin. She came at Christmas, a year and a half after he visited her, and stayed with him in the flat in Terenure, sleeping with him, a rather distant, very erect, somewhat pinched-looking middle-aged woman whom he met on a railway platform after she'd come from Belfast, lots of make-up on her and her hands on a handbag in front of a claret coat. She looked initially like some child's aunt from Barna Craugh; she was, ironically, a face from the main street of that town but with the days the reserve, the austerity, the fear even went and something trying to get out of Joly for years re-emerged, at first tokens, a Barna Craugh rasp in the accent, the desert-storm of freckles on the face becoming suddenly plainer – it was the beauty queen. With passion Joly became younger, vulnerable. She was going into marriage with Colin Lysaght again. In a state of vulnerability, of protective layers thrown away, she was stepping out of her world and going into Colin's again. She was leaving children and the intermediary years of exile, of flight behind. She was returning to a country that had changed, exposing herself to that country again.

She didn't know what she was doing with this man who had in a way ruined her life, walking down O'Connell Street with him, but there seemed to be an inevitability, an order about them being together; this time he was the protector, he was the guide of an innerly crippled person; he was bound to her by guilt. Such were the vicissitudes of life she thought, passing a go-go dancing model in Cleary's window, that people should merge into a marriage again, brought about by guilt in one partner, now healed and whole, over the last marriage. Such was the ongoing nature of a lunatic marriage and maybe they had to find love in it to make it easier for both of them. The beauty queen and the vicar might not prove such a bad match after all.

But what immediately kept Joly going, down O'Connell Street, was fascination with the person beside her, the difference in him, the wholeness. A hurricane had gone through him and created a new person. There was ultimately, as in the first marriage, amazement and humility that this person should be interested in her. A recognition of her roots in Bin Lane and a renewed vision of them breaking from her in a flurry of distraught Easter doves, which made everything all right, pain, exile, solitude. Ultimately she was the little girl from Bin Lane who broke the rules and won, however it was done, however afflicted was the course in doing it, the heart of the obese and beaming town councillor. For the renewed hallucination of doves tearing away from an inchoate source, for the life-reinvigorating sensation of it – probably the same sensation young people in Edinburgh got from sniffing glue – she returned to Ireland. She groped her way back blindly. And the person who met her again was equally blind in guilt and in grief, looking over her shoulder at Amiens Street Station and seeing the person he knew she would obliterate forever this time, his father hanging from a roof beam. Or would she? Either way that image was subdued now, like an old war-flag in a Protestant church. He kissed her and asked her about the children she'd left in Scotland. It was spring. Three months since he'd last seen her. He took her baggage and carried it towards their new life together, an arc of light in the rainy sky you could see through the station-bar window, like a strand of grey hair over the eye.

8

Colin gave up his job and purchased a gate-lodge in the countryside near the vicarage, with money left over from selling the vicarage and the Lysaght town house. He got a job, after some training, on a forestry near the gate-lodge. A new job for him, one that initially amazed the locals. Then they let him be. Joly went back to live near the town she grew up in, still very much a Protestant, growing nasturtiums, geraniums, chrysanthemums, goldenrod, marrows, braving the country that tried to destroy her. She didn't let it destroy her again. She didn't let it in on her. A new flush came to Colin's cheek. They seemed happy, an odd pair who didn't mix much, alone in a gate-lodge in a countryside of ghosts, ghosts of rural vicarages, of eccentric, set-back Ascendancy mansions that now looked out on thriving Free State forestry plantations, on the cars that sped on these back-roads, bringing young couples to discos, on the nerve of change at last in this atavistic and laden green air.

When a statue of the Virgin Mary by a roadway was reckoned to have moved there was no hullabaloo, just smiles, and Joly was reminded of the time as a child she dressed up as Our Lady of Fatima for local children and played that part, in a shed, appearing on a stage of fragile boards. When this image returned to her she knew she'd changed once more; it was autumn, the nasturtiums ran through the garden in glittering rivers; a sort of miracle had happened; the Catholic and Protestant parts of her had merged as she remembered a very jocose Our Lady of Fatima, her veil slipping off, her hands joined in prayer and redcurrant, gleaming lipstick smeared on her lips that, try as they could, couldn't hold back a luscious, cherubic smile.

Miles

'Miles from here.' A phrase caught Miles's ear as he took the red bus to the North Wall. Someone was shouting at someone else, one loud passenger at an apparently half-deaf passenger, the man raising himself a little to shout. The last of Dublin's bright lights swam by. What took their place was the bleak area of dockland. Miles took his small case from the bus. He had a lonely and unusual journey to make.

Miles was seventeen. His hair was manically spliced on his head, a brown tuft of it. He was tall, lean; Miles was a model. He wore his body comfortably. He moved ahead to the boat, carrying his case: foisting his case in an onward movement.

Miles had grown up in the Liberties in Dublin. His mother had deserted him when he was very young. She was a red-haired legend tonight, a legend with a head of champion-chestnut hair.

She had gone from Ireland and insinuated herself into England, leaving her illegitimate son with her married sister. The only thing known of her was that she turned up at the pilgrimage to Walsingham, Norfolk, each year. Miles, now that he was a spare-featured seventeen-year-old, a seventeen-year-old with a rather lunar face, was going looking for her. That lunar face was even paler now under the glare of lights from the boat.

The life Miles lived now was one of bright lights, of outlandish clothes, of acrobatic models wearing those clothes under the glare of acrobatic lights; more than anything it was a life of nightclubs, the later in the night the better, seats at lurid

141

feasts of mosaic icecream and of cocktails. Dublin for Miles was a kind of Pompeii now: on an edge. He was doing well, he was living a good life in a city smouldering with poverty. Ironically he'd come from want. But his good looks had brought him to magazines and to the omnipotent television screen. He was taking leave of all that for a few days for a pilgrimage of his own. There were few signs of garishness on him. The clothes he slipped out of Ireland in were black and grey. Only the articulate outline of his face and the erupting lava tuft of his hair would let you know he worked in the world of modelling.

The night-boat pulled him towards England and the world of his mother.

2

She'd come to Walsingham each year, Ellie, and this year there was a difference about her coming. She was dying. She came with her daughter Áine and with her son Lally. She walked, propped between them, on the pilgrimage, the procession on foot from slipper chapel to town of Walsingham, Áine was a teacher. Lally was a pop star.

3

Miles was in fact late for the procession. He arrived in the town when the crowds were jumbled together. He looked around. He looked through the crowd for his mother.

4

Afterwards you could almost say that Lally recognized him, rather than he recognized Lally. Lally was discomfited by lack of recognition here. Miles recognized him immediately. 'How are you? You're Lally.' A primrose and white religious banner made one or two demonstrative movements behind Miles.

'Yea. And who are you?'

Who am I? Who am I? The question, coming from Lally's lips,

funnelled mesmerically into Miles's mind on that street in Walsingham.

5

Miles was an orphan, always an orphan, always made to feel like an orphan. He was, through childhood and adolescence, rejected by his cousins with whom he lived, both male and female, rejected for his beauty. Nancy Boy they called him. Sop. Cissy. Pansy. Queer, Gay-Boy, Bum-Boy. The ultimate name – Snowdrop. His enemy cousins took to that name most, considering it particularly salacious and inventive. Miles was none of these things. He looked unusually pretty for a boy. The names for him and the brand of ostracization gave him a clue as to his direction in life though. He found as easy entrance into the world of modelling. He was hoisted gracefully into that world you could say. At seventeen Miles had his face right bang on the front of magazine covers. He'd become an aura, a national consciousness arrangement in his own right. This success allowed him to have a flat of his own and, supreme revenge, wear suits the colour of the undersides of mushrooms down the Liberties. Miles sometimes had the blank air of a drifting, unpiloted boat in these suits in the Liberties. There must be more to life than bright suits his mind was saying; there must be things beyond this city where boys in pink suits wandered under slender cathedral steeples. There must be more to life than a geography that got its kicks from mixing ancient grey buildings with doses of alarmingly dressed and vacant-eyed young people. His mother, the idea of her, was something beyond this city and Miles broke with everything he was familiar with, everything that bolstered him, to go looking for her, to stretch his life: to endanger himself. He knew his equilibrium was frail, that his defences were thin, that he might inflict a terrible wound on himself by going, that he might remember what he'd been trying to forget all his life, what it was like as a little child to have your mother leave you, to have a red-haired woman disappear out the door, throwing a solitary backward glance at you, in a house not far from the slender cathedral steeple, and never coming back again.

6

Who am I? Ellie Tierney had asked herself as she walked on the procession. Who am I, she wondered, now that she was on the verge of dying, having cancer of the bone marrow. An immigrant. A mother of two children. A widow. A grocery store owner. A dweller of West London. A Catholic.

She'd come young to this country; from County Clare. Just before the war. Lived the first year in Ilford. Had shoals of local children pursue her and her brothers and sisters with stones because they were Irish. She'd been a maid in a vast hotel. Met Peader Tierney, a bus driver for London Transport, had a proposal from him at a Galwaymen's ball in a West London hotel and married him. Had two children by him. Was independent of him in that she opened a grocery store of her own. He'd died in the early 1970s, long before he could see his son become famous.

7

Who am I? Lally had thought on the procession. The question boggled him now. He was very famous. Frequently on television. A spokesman for a new generation of the Irish in England. A wearer of nightgown-looking shirts. He felt odd, abashed here, among the nuns and priests, beside his mother. But he strangely belonged. He'd make a song from Walsingham.

8

Who am I? Áine had thought as she'd walked. A failure. A red-haired woman in a line of Clare women. Beside that young brother of hers nothing: a point of annihilation, no achievement.

9

It occurred to Lally that Miles had come here because he knew that he, Lally, would be here. Lally welcomed him as a particularly devoted fan.

'Where are you from?'

'Dublin.'

'Dublin?'

'Dublin.'

The hair over Miles's grin was askew. Miles waited a few minutes, grin fixed, for a further comment from Lally.

'We're driving to the sea. Will you come with us?'

10

The flat land of Norfolk: not unlike the sea. The onward Volkswagen giving it almost an inconsequential, disconnected feel; a feel that brought dreams and memories to those sitting, as if dumbstruck, silently in the car. Mrs Tierney in front, her face searching the sky with the abstracted look of a saint who had his hands joined in prayer. Walsingham was left behind. But the spirit of Walsingham bound all the car together, this strangeness in a landscape that was otherwise yawning, and to Irish people, alien, unremarkable – important only in that it occasionally yielded an odd-looking bird and that the glowering sweep of it promised the maximum benefit of the sea.

That they all considered it flat and boundless like the sea never occurred to them as being ironic; a sea of land was something almost to be feared. Only by the sea, in landscape, they felt safe.

Or in a small town like Walsingham which took full control over its surroundings and subjugated them.

The people of Britain had called the Milky Way the Walsingham Way once. They thought it had led to Walsingham. The Virgin Mary was reckoned to have made an appearance here in the Middle Ages. The young Henry the Eighth had walked on foot from the slipper chapel to her shrine to venerate her. Later he'd taken her image from the shrine and had it publicly burned in Chelsea to the jeers of a late-medieval crowd. Centuries had gone by and an English lady convert started the process of reconstruction, turning sheds back into chapels. To celebrate the reconsecration of the slipper chapel vast crowds had come from all over England on a Whit Monday in the 1930s. Ellie remembered the Whit Monday gathering here 1946, the crowds on the procession, the prayers of thanksgiving to Mary, the nuns with head-dresses tall as German castles, pictures of Mary in windows in Walsingham and the flowers on doorsteps – a gaggle of nuns in black, but with palatial white head-dresses, standing outside a cottage, nudging one another, waiting for the Virgin as if she was a military hero who'd won the war. The statue of Mary had come, bedecked with congratulatory pink roses. For Ellie the war had been a war with England, English children chasing her and brutally raining stones on her.

Her head slumped in the car a little now: she was tired. Her son, Lally, the driver, looked sidelong at her, anxiously, protectively. Her memories were his this moment: the stuff of songs, geese setting out like rebel soldiers in a jade-green farm in County Clare.

11

Lally was the artist, the pop star, the maker of words. Words came out of him now, these days, like meteors; superhuman ignitions of energy. He was totally in command: he stood straight on television. He was a star. He was something of Ireland for a new generation of an English pop audience. He wheedled his songs about Ireland into a microphone, the other members of his group standing behind him. His face was well known in teeny-bop magazines, the alacrity of it, the upright-ness of it.

How all this came about was a mystery to his mother; from a shambles in a shed, a pop group practising, to massive concerts – a song in the charts was what did it. But a song with a difference. It was a song about Ireland. Suddenly Ireland had value in the media. Lally had capitalized on that. His sore-throat-sounding songs had homed in on that new preoccupation.

Without people realizing it he had turned a frivolous interest into an obsession. He remembered – through his parents. His most famous song was about his father, how his father, who'd fled Galway in his teens, had returned, middle-aged, to find only stones where his parents were buried, no names on the stones. It had never occurred to him that without him, the son of the family, there'd been no one to bury his parents. He had a mad sister somewhere in England who talked to chickens. Lally's father had deserted the entire palette of Ireland for forty years, never once writing to his parents when they were alive, trying to obliterate the memory of them, doing so until he found his way home again in the late 1960s.

That song had been called 'Stones in a Flaxen Field'.

Words; Lally was loved for his words. They spun from him, all colours. They were sexual and male and young, his words. They were kaleidoscopic in colour. But they spoke, inversely, of things very ancient, of oppression. A new generation of young English people learnt from his songs.

And only ten years before, Ellie often thought, her grocery store was stoned, one night, just after bombs went off in Birmingham, the window all smashed.

Ah well; that was life. That was change. One day scum, the next stars. Stars . . . Ellie looked up from her dreams for the Milky Way or the Walsingham Way but it was still very much May late-afternoon light.

12

Her father told her how they used to play hurling in the fields outside his village in County Galway in May evening light, 'light you could cup in your hand it was so golden'. There are holes in every legend. There were two versions of her father. The man who ran away and who never went back until he was in his fifties. And the man who'd proposed to her mother at a Galwayman's ball. 'But sure he was only there as a spy that day,' Áine's mother would always say. Even so it was contradictory. Áine resented the lyricism of Lally's version of her father; she resented the way he'd used family and put it into song, she resented this intrusion into the part of her psyche which was wrapped up in family. More than anything she resented the way Lally got away with it. But still she outwardly applauded him. But as he became more famous she became older, more wrecked looking. Still her hair was very red. That seemed to be her triumph – even at school. To have this almost obscenely lavish red hair. She got on well at school. She had many boyfriends. Too many. She was involved on women's committees. But wasn't there something she'd lost?

She did not believe in all this: God, pilgrimage. Coming to Walsingham almost irked her. She'd come as a duty. But it did remind her of another pilgrimage, another journey, almost holy.

13

It had been when Lally was a teenager. She'd gone for an abortion in Brighton. A clinic near the sea. In winter. He'd accompanied her. Waiting for the appointment she'd heard the crash of the winter sea. Lally beside her. He'd held her hand. She'd thought of Clare, of deaths, of wakes. She'd gone in for her appointment. Afterwards, in a strange way, she realized he'd become an artist that day. By using him as a solace when he'd been too young she'd traumatized him into becoming an artist. She'd wanted him to become part of a conspiracy with her, a narrow conspiracy: but instead she'd sent him out on seas of philosophizing, of wondering. He'd been generous in his interpretation of her from out on those seas. His purity not only had been reinforced but immeasurably extended. While hers was lost.

There'd been a distance between them ever since. Lally was the one whose life worked, Lally was the one with the pop star's miraculous sweep of dark hair over his face, Lally was the one with concise blue eyes that carried the Clare coast in them.

Today she saw it exactly. Lally was the one who believed.

14

Miles was so chuffed at being in this company that he said nothing; he just grinned. He hid his head, slightly idiotically, in his coat. The countryside rolled by outside. All the time he was aware of the journey separating him from his quest for his mother. But he didn't mind. When it came to the point it had seemed futile, the idea of finding her in that crowd. And romantic. When he looked out from a porch, near a pump, at the sea of faces, it had seemed insane, deranged, dangerous, the point of his quest. There'd been a moment when he thought his sanity was giving way. But the apparition of Lally had saved him. Now he was being swept along on another odyssey. But where was this odyssey leading? And as he was on it, the car journey, it was immediately bringing him to thoughts, memories. The landscape of adolescence, the stretched-out skyline of Dublin, a naked black river bearing isolated white lights at night as it meandered drunkenly to the no man's land, the unclaimed territory of the Irish Sea. This was the territory along with the terrain of the black river as it neared the sea which infiltrated Miles's night-dreams as an adolescent, restive night-dreams, his body shaking frequently in response to the image of the Irish Sea at night, possibly knowing it had to enter that image so it could feel whole, Miles knowing, even in sleep, that the missing mechanisms of his being were out there and recoiling, in a few spasmodic movements, from the journey he knew he'd have to make some day. He was on that journey now. But he'd already left the focus of it, Walsingham. What had come in place of Walsingham was flat land, an unending succession of flat land which seemed to induce a mutual, binding memory to the inmates of the car. A memory which hypnotized everybody.

But the memory which was special to Miles was the memory of Dublin. This memory had a new intensity, a new aurora in the presence of Lally; the past was changed in the presence of Lally and newly negotiated. Miles had found, close to Lally, new fundamentals in his past; the past seemed levitated, random, creative now. Miles knew now that all the pain in his life had been going towards this moment. This was the reward. It was as if Miles, the fourteen year, fifteen-year-old, had smashed out of his body and, like superman, stormed the sky over a city. The city was a specific one. Dublin. And remembering a particular corner near his aunt's home where there was always the sculpture of some drunkard's piddle on the wall Miles was less euphoric. The world was made up of mean things after all, mornings after the night before. That's what Miles's young life was made up of, mornings after the night before. Maybe that's what his mother's life had been like too. Now that he was moving further and further away from the possibility of actually finding her he could conjure an image of her he hadn't dared conjure before. He could conjure an encounter with her which, in the presence of an artist, Lally, was a hair's breadth away from being real.

15

Rose Keating had set out that morning from her room in Shepherd's Bush. She was a maid in a Kensington hotel where most of the staff were Irish. Her hair, which was almost the colour of golden nasturtiums, was tied in a ponytail at the back. Her pale face looked earnest. She made this journey every year. She made it in a kind of reparation. She always felt early on this journey that her womb had been taken out, that there was a missing segment of her, an essential ion in her consciousness was lost. She'd almost forgotten, living in loneliness and semi-destitution, who she was and why she was here. All she knew, instinctively, all the time was that she'd had to move on. There had been a child she'd had once and she'd abandoned him because she didn't want to drag him down her road too. She felt, when she'd left Dublin, totally corrupt, totally spoilt. She'd wanted to cleanse herself and just ended up a maid, a dormant being, a piece of social trash.

There was a time when it was as if any man would do her but the more good-looking the better: at night a chorus of silent young men gathered balletically under lamp-posts in the Liberties. Then there was a play, movements, interchange. Which would she choose? She looked as though she'd been guided like a robot towards some of them. All this under lamplight. Her face slightly thrown back and frequently expressionless. There was something wrong with her, people said, she had a disease, 'down there', and some matrons even pointed to the place. Rose loved the theatre of it. There was something *mardi gras* about picking up young men. My gondoliers she called them mentally. Because sometimes she didn't in fact see young men from the Liberties under lamp-posts but Venetian gondoliers; the Liberties was often studded with Venetian gondoliers and jealous women, behind black masks, looked from windows. Rose had a mad appetite, its origins and its name inscrutable, for men. There was no point of reference for it so it became a language, fascinating in itself. Those with open minds wanted to study that language to see what new things they could learn from it. No one in Ireland was as sexually insatiable as Rose. This might have been fine if she'd been a prostitute but she didn't even get money for it very often; she just wanted to put coloured balloons all over a panoramic, decayed, Georgian ceiling that was in fact the imaginative ceiling of Irish society.

It was a phase. It hit her, like a moonbeam, in her late teens, and it lasted until her mid-twenties. She got a son out of it, Miles, and the son made her recondite, for a while, and then she went back to her old ways, the streets. But this time each man she had seemed tainted and diseased after her, a diseased, invisible mucus running off him and making him curl up with horror at the awareness of this effect. He had caught something incurable and he hated himself for it. He drifted away from her, trying to analyse what felt different and awful about him. Sex had turned sour, like the smell of Guinness sometimes in the Dublin air.

But Rose, even living with her sister, could not give it up; her whole body was continually infiltrated by sexual hunger and one day, feeling sick in herself, she left. The day she left Dublin she thought of a red-haired boy, the loveliest she had, who'd ended up spending a life sentence in Mountjoy, for a murder of a rural garda sergeant, having hit him over the head one night in the Liberties, with a mallet. He'd been half a tinker and wore mousy freckles at the tip of his nose – like a tattoo.

London had ended all her sexual appetite: it took her dignity; it made her middle-aged. But it never once made her want to return. She held her child in her head, a talisman, and she went to Walsingham once a year as a reparation, having sent a postcard from there once to her sister, saying: 'If you want to find me, find me in Walsingham.' That had been at a moment of piqued desperation. She'd written the postcard on a wall beside a damp telephone kiosk and the postcard itself became damp; people, happy people, sauntering, with chips, around her.

For a few years she found a companion for her trip to Walsingham, a Mr Coneelly, a bald man from the hotel, a hat on his head on the pilgrimage, a little earthenware leprechaun grin on his face under his hat. He had an amorous attachment to her. There was always a ten-pound note sticking from his pocket and a gold chain trailing to the watch in that pocket. But the romance ended when white rosary beads fell out of his trousers pocket as he was making love to her once on a shabby, once lustrous gold sofa, she doing it to be obliging, and he taking the falling rosary as a demonstration by his dead mother against the romance. In fact he found a much younger girl after that and he made sure no rosary fell from his pocket in the middle of making love. He had been company, for a while.

Rose had geared herself for a life of loneliness. Today in Walsingham it rained a little and she stood to the side, on a porch, and watched.

16

Sometimes Áine's feelings towards her brother came to hatred. She never pretended it. She was always courteous, even decorous with him: the worst and the most false of her, 'school-mistressly'. She resented his strident, bulbous shirts, the free movements of those shirts, the colours of them. She resented what he did with experience, turning it into an artifact. Artifacts weren't life and yet, for him, they created a life of their own: those Botticelli angels looking at him from an audience, full of adulation. Áine wanted reports on life to be factual, plain; Lally, the Irish artist, threw the facts into tumults of colour where they got distorted. Eventually the words took on a frenzy, a life of their own. They were able to change the miserable facts – rain over a desultory, praying horde at Walsingham, crouched in

between Chinese take-aways – and turn themselves into something else, a miracle, a transcendence, an elevation and an
obliviscence: wine turned into the blood of Christ at mass. A
mergence with all the Irish artists of the centuries. Of course
Lally was only a pop star and yet his words, she had to admit
sometimes, were as truthful as any Irish writer's. His words
exploded on concert stages, on television and told of broken
Irish lives, red-haired Irish women immigrants who worked in
hotels in West London.

17

Miles had stood not very far away from his mother that day
and Lally had noticed Miles's mother, when there was rain, as
she stood talking to two men from Mayo. There was a hullabaloo of Irish accents between Rose and the two men from
Mayo. Lally paused; a story. Then he went on. Miles didn't tell
Lally in the car that he'd come in search of a red-haired
woman. He said very little and was asked very little.

18

Rose, sheltering her body from the rain, got into a livid conversation with two men. They were bachelors and they were both
looking for wives. They came to Walsingham, Norfolk, from
Birmingham each Whit Monday looking for wives and they
went to Lisdoonvarna, County Clare, in September looking for
wives. So far they'd had no luck and their quest was telling on
them: their hair and their teeth were falling out. One bandied a
copy of the previous day's *Sunday Press* as if it was the port-
folio of his life's work.

'And do you have a husband?' one of them asked.

'What do you think?'

'You've had your share of fellas,' the other one said, grin-
ning, 'A woman like you wouldn't have gone without a man
for long.'

'What do you mean. A woman like me?'

'Well, you're not fat but you've loads of flesh on you. Like a Christmas goose. That's not derogatory. You look as firm as my grandmother's armchair.'

Rose screeched with laughter.

'And you both look as though the hinges are coming out of you.'

'Mentally or in the body.'

Rose laughed again.

'Whatever hope there is in Clare there's no hope here. Unless you want a Reverend Mother.'

'O you'd be surprised.' A twinkle in the eye. 'Lots of randy women go on pilgrimages.'

19

Nearing the sea as though it was the Atlantic Ocean that blanketed the west coast of Ireland all kinds of words and images came into the head of Lally, the driver: sentences, half-heard at Irish venues – music festivals, Irish ballrooms – and elaborated on by him. So they could take their place in a narrative song. But more than words and images came now – an apotheosis came too. Lally was flying with the success and daring of his life. He was proud of himself. He'd turned something of the decrepitude and semi-stagnation of his parents' lives into art. More than that. Art for the young. He'd dolled his ancestry up in fancy dress.

20

How many days and months would she have to live? Ellie thought of Clare where she'd been born, the harvest fields there she'd walked before leaving Ireland, those blond, human fields, warm after days of summer sun. The imminence of death brought the friendliest images of her life.

21

The bastard, Áine thought, the bastard, he's taken everything that was of my creativity; he's used up my creativity. He's left me as nothing. There's no more to go around. He's a man, an exploiter, a rampant egotist. He doesn't see who he's trampled on to get where he's got, who he hurts. He doesn't see he's squashed my self-confidence out.

22

For Miles, as they neared sea, it was a trip backwards: at least this journey, this expedition to Walsingham had allowed him to be solemn about his life, to see it: he sat back as though his life hitherto, as he could see it, was a state funeral.

There had been state funerals he'd seen in his life. De Valera's, for instance, which he'd seen with his aunt. 'Ah, sure, look at his coffin.' All kinds of voices came back from Miles's life. Especially, the voices of early adolescence. 'Ah, sure look at the little eigit. The fool. Nitwit. Silly Git.' All kinds of names were planted on Miles's always withdrawing figure with its gander legs in thin jeans. That figure was a continual epilogue, always disappearing around corners, always on the edge of getting out of the picture. But maybe that was because he knew there'd be an area where he could totally affirm himself, totally show himself – when the time came. Now there were ikons of Miles in fashion magazines, the young archangel in suave clothes. His tormentors in the Liberties would be bilious. But the young man in the picture was unmoved by this prospect. He seemed frigid of countenance. This loveliness was the product of pain. These secretive eyes in all the pictures looked back on tunnels of streets in the Liberties, streets where his mother had gathered men as if they'd been daisies.

As they neared Wells-next-the-Sea the sky, towards evening, had almost cleared and there were a few white clouds in it – like defeated daisies.

People in the car were mumbling, conversations were going on. Suddenly Miles wanted to go back to Walsingham. 'Mammy.'

23

Rose's shadow departed through the back door after her. Miles should have known there was something funny about her going that day. In fact he did know. Memory consolidated that fact. Rose's shadow writhed off a yellowy picture showing military-shouldered women in white, straw hats on their heads, holding bicycles, in some Edwardian wood of the Dublin mountains.

24

'And the queer thing is that Gabrielle knew Marty years before in Kiltimagh.'

Rose was in a Chinese restaurant in Walsingham with the two immigrants who were originally from Mayo. They'd discovered they had an acquaintance in common; a partisan in this tide of menial, immigrant Irish labour. Rose had encountered her in a hotel room once where the carpets had been rolled up after some VIP visitors had spent a lengthy stay. The room, grandiose in proportions, was being renovated. Rose did not know what to dwell on, the conversation with the two odd men or the drama of the encounter years before. Her concentration ultimately flitted between the figment of now and the thought of then. This caused an almost clownish agitation in her features.

'She had the devil of a temper.'

'O yes, she'd flare up at you like a snake.'

'There was cuddling in her though.'

'You dirty . . .'

Rose's mind had fled the banter between the two men. A woman in a hotel room in London years before, a blue work-coat on her, a conversation, commiseration, companionship then for a few months. But some family tragedy had brought the women back to Ireland and then Rose never saw her again; no more Friday evenings over a candle-lit, hard-as-a-horseshoe pizza in Hammersmith.

'Go on out of that. Don't be disparaging a woman's reputation. She's not around to defend herself.'

Rose's mind had drifted. She could see the sea, the grey sea such as it was piled up, a mute and undemonstrative statement, around Dublin and longed for it as though it had the confessional's power of absolution.

25

Miles stumbled by the sea. A few boats there, backs up. Now it was grey again, an overall grey. Walking done, the group went to a seaside café.

26

Words, they're my story, they're my life. Here by the sea, dusk, the jukebox going, Dusty Springfield, 'I just don't know what to do with myself', no song of mine on the jukebox. Chips, a boy, already tanned, looking from behind the counter, mystically, a Spaniard's or a Greek's black moustache on him. I'll make another song, another story. Stories will get me by, words, won't they, won't they? The stage, the lights, the mammoth audience. Is this a Nazi dream of power?

27

Today the religion they tried to kill. My religion. Remember when Peader and I went to the Church of the English Martyrs in Tyburn and we, privately, consecrated our marriage there on the site where the head of Oliver Plunkett, the Irish martyr, was chopped off, the nuns all singing, white on them. What will it be like to be dead? – back in that dream of a hymn sung in unison by nuns in white where Irish bishops in the long ago met their deaths.

28

Lally went obsessively, again and again, to the jukebox, standing over it, putting on more songs as though lighting candles in a bed of church candles. Midsummer dusk was out there, the strangeness of it. A woman soon to die looked at it. Lally's backside was very blue.

29

Loneliest of all was Miles, the stranger here, the one picked up
and talked to as if being picked up was favour enough or as if he
was supposed to sit in silent wonderment. He was an oddity
from the sea of fans. He was an orphan among these people
who, in a strange, unknowing way, patronized him.

30

The strangeness, the awkwardness became more evident as the
number of coffees coming to the table multiplied, each set of
coffees being ushered in more frenetically than the last. No one
told their story aloud or was asked to.

31

Rose, though, was telling her story very loudly indeed not many
miles away. Sweet and sour chicken, a plate of it, went by as she
got to the part about leaving Ireland. Her immediate listeners
were enthralled but their wonderment was more at how gauche
exiles very often hid the most amazing secrets, how they hid
horror, terror and great magnitudes of sin – incest, homosexuality, lesbianism, prostitution, now, rare enough, nymphomania.
England dusted off the sins and made people just foolish – just
foolish Irish folk.

'The child? The little lad?'

'Sure he's grown now. He wouldn't want to see me.'

32

O Mother of God, Star of the Sea, pray for us, pray that we find
loved ones. Someone's limbs to get caught up with in a mildly
comfortable bed.

Lally remembered, from childhood, a Sacred Heart picture
over the bed of a dying, bald uncle, a gay uncle who had a
festive chamber-pot under his death bed, a chamber-pot with

crocks of gold running around it. Before AIDS was invented,
that uncle seemed to be dying of something like AIDS. Or
maybe merely an overdose of failure, an overdose of incohesion.
His version of Ireland didn't merge with England.

The harvest fields of Clare didn't get him by here: England
scoured him. England debilitated him. England killed his spirit
and then killed him. But not before he carried on a kind of
maudlin homosexuality. The white hands of a corpse Lally saw,
a rosary entwined in them, had been lain on his genitalia when
he was a child, a St Stephen's Day Christmas tree behind the
merry lecher, other people gone to bed.

Ireland kicked up such stories like sand in your feet on a
beach: Ireland was so full of sadness. Ireland fed itself into
Lally's songs now. They came out, these stories, renewed,
revitalized, pop songs for a generation who swayed and
sometimes jived to them and couldn't be unnerved by them.

Star of the Sea, pray for the wanderer, pray for me. Lally's
blue-shirted wrist wrestled with a bottle of Coke now. He was
on to Coke. And he being the pop star, everyone watched the
movement of his wrist, everybody's attention had gone to his
wrist in alarm, people realizing that they'd been neglecting Lally
for a while and that his wrist was telling them so.

And despite resenting him a little maybe they were glad for
the coherence he gave to something of their lives. Even to death.

'Beach at Brighton, Baby-death.' Áine was looking at her
brother in stillness now, not in anger or resentment.

33

As stars came out they walked on the beach. Lally tried to
identify the stars in the sky. The Walsingham Way? Next week
he'd be in California. By the Pacific. Watching the sky of stars
over the Pacific. But he'd take something from here. Pointers to
his mother's life and death. Ellie too saw her life and death in
the stars tonight. A constellation of stars like a constellation of
wheat fields in County Clare. 'A time to plant and a time to
pluck up that which is planted.' Áine saw London classrooms in
the sky, children of many races, rivers of children's faces. Miles,

away from the group, dissociated from it, didn't look at the stars but poked the sea with a stick.

34

'Goodbye to yis all now.' Drunk, unpilgrim-like, Rose tottered out of a pub near the Chinese restaurant in Walsingham, looking behind at a constellation of lights in the window of that pub that might have distinguished it as a brothel if it had been in a city. The lovers stood at the door, goodbyes in their eyes. They were bent on returning, getting *stociously* drunk and staying the night in Walsingham. A bus would take Rose home. Her hair down on her shoulders she was a manifestation of Irishness in her dowdy coat. Her back stooped a little: she was an aged pilgrim. The successive pilgrimages were gradations, demarcations of age. But there was a wicked youthfulness about the way she stepped on the bus and turned around, shouting back to the men who hadn't yet gone back into the pub. 'Up Mayo.' Bandy knees afar twitched in response to her salutation: two Mayo bachelors looked suddenly spectral, looked like a vision in a wash of white light from a turning car. Then they were gone, gone into the album.

35

In the middle of summer in Wells-next-the-Sea there would be boys with faces pugnaciously browned by sun, boys whose crotches would be held in by aerial blue jeans, battalions of these boys unleashed on the place and their eyes, the explosive look in their eyes, turning the nights into a turmoil. Boats would be lined up on the beach. Lanes would meander down to the beach as they did now. The jukeboxes would be more active. England would come here to be loved, ladies from Birmingham, factory boys, boys with backsides tight and fecund as plums. This is where England would take a few weeks off, the boring country of England becoming carnal, becoming daring, becoming poetic. Caution and pairs of cheap nylon stockings would be thrown to the nervy summer breezes. The grey would go for a few weeks, making room for a blue that visited the place from the deep Mediterranean.

Ellie would be dead in July. Her funeral would be in West London on a very hot day. Áine would cry more than anybody. Lally would be silent, a pop star in black and white, no tie, white *fin de siècle* shirt spaciously open in the cemetery. There'd be a red rose in his black lapel. The sun would be gruesomely hot. Áine would be crying for a country she never really knew, a country for which her red hair was an emblem.

Miles would start losing his soul that summer, if soul you could call it; his sensitivity, vulnerability, belief in something. Walsingham and Wells-next-the-Sea would have been the last stops for his openness. After that, though still in media terms outrageously beautiful, he'd start becoming hard, calculating, eyes, those brown eyes of his, focused on attainment. All he'd want to do would to be a star and oblivionize, kill anything else in him. There'd be no sign of Rose in this Italian suit dolled-up boy.

36

Rose let herself in the hall door. 14 Bolingbroke Road, Shepherd's Bush, London. Inside the light wasn't working. The smell of urine came from the first-floor toilet. She was a little drunk still. Her drunken form merged with the darkness. The smell of urine was aquatic in the air the further she walked in. But the darkness was benign to her. It shrouded her unhappiness, the unhappiness which had suddenly come on her in the bus as she remembered what she'd been trying to forget for years, what she'd been successfully putting Walsingham between it and her for years. Now pilgrimages, trips to Walsingham, the cabbalistic charades of them and the inexact hope they gave off didn't work any more and all she could see, right in front of her, was the greyness, the no-hope, the lethargy land of *it*.

37

The lights of a motorway going back to London and the lights rearing up at you, daisy trails of them. Four silent people in the car, one sleeping, the strange boy, a phrase coming to Lally's head as he drove, a phrase he wouldn't use in a song, an unwelcome phrase even. It came from a prayer of his mother's he remembered from childhood.

'And after this our exile.'

By the River

'Gregory.' Nóra's voice came out of the dark. 'Gregory.'

I was standing in the dark, at the entrance to the dining room. She had entered from the doorway which led to the kitchen.

She'd said my name a third time. This time her voice faltered a bit. I had heard that night that she was going to die. She knew I'd heard. I'd come most of all out of a sense of betrayal that her life was going to be curtailed. She was my real mother – imaginatively; Nóra was the benefactress of my foolishnesses, Nóra was my best friend.

A tall woman moved in the dark by the doorway, a quirky movement, like a troubled reflection on water.

'Nóra.' I ran towards her. That night I dreamt we were both going down in water, the black water of the river beside the town, into which many mental hospital patients, male and female, had jumped in their pantomime pyjamas.

My mother woke me with some rancour on her face in the morning. There was sweat all over me like florets of ice on a winter window.

2

'Now pet, give us that performance again.'

I was dressed as Our Lady of Fatima, a white bath towel over me. I emulated the Virgin Mary in one of her appearances in Fatima, stepping out from behind a dried-looking yellow ochre curtain.

'Repent or ye'll all perish.'

Nóra was with an obese young man who worked for the circus visiting the town at that moment, a voluminous, grey suit hanging in anarchic folds on him. In a way he was disinherited from the circus, never staying in caravans, always sojourning with Nóra during the circus's visit to town. He was a son of one of the bosses. His exact job was difficult to say but he painted illustrations on caravans; he led baby alligators, through the fair green, on strings, still in the voluminous, the cosmopolitan disparity of that suit.

'And what do we have to repent for?' The young man's slightly girlish, slightly ringing voice suddenly cut in, a shaft of whiskey-coloured hair standing on the top of his head which promised forthcoming baldness.

'Enslavement to lust,' I said.

'Heck,' the guy spluttered to Nóra, 'Give me lust any time even if it means damnation.'

Nóra seemed to interpret some hidden meaning in that sentiment, looking at him with a glee that melted the few freckles on her cheeks and turned the ends of her hair into a momentary, friendly auburn haze.

I was peeved by a sense of exclusion and immediately, in my capacity as the Virgin Mary, threw a tantrum, screaming threats at the imaginary, unfortunate children who were supposed to be witnessing this apparition, the lambs they were tending running away in terror in the ever-available cinema of my mind's eye.

When I got home that evening I went to sleep to a dream of evening over Fatima, sunset on fields where less frightened lambs grazed and a Virgin Mary, in white, with a pale blue sash hanging down her leg wandered, waiting to be noticed.

3

Nóra threw a party for local children, having none of her own. Nóra's reputation had gone down a little lately: people muttered about her and the circus man. Only the children of pub owners came and the unique children of an engineer visiting the town for a few months from Dublin, helping to set up a local

electricity generating plant. These children were Lemon and
Marmalade because, twin girls, one had lemon hair and the
other marmalade hair, though their curls and waves, now that
the girls were nine years old, were in danger of running into
other ravishing and less easy to distinguish colours.

Lemon sang a song 'Boolavogue' which she learnt from a
strongly republican Dublin grandfather, her hands behind her
pink cardigan, and the daughter of Kelly, the pub owner at the
curve of Trophy Street and Bridge Street, belted out 'The Bells of
the Angelus are calling to Pray, Ave, Ave.' A fat cousin of mine
sneaked into the congregation at a late hour, though he wasn't
supposed to be here, coming in the front door from which you
could always fetch a key through the letter-box on an old brown
string, and he started staring in fixation at Nóra, he too having
heard she was going to die. I was here, I was allowed Nóra's
company, simply because my mother was in hospital. She'd
been in hospital a lot recently, getting bouts of a mysterious
illness. My cousin's stare became apparent to everybody after a
while and there was a pool of space around Nóra, as if
facilitating my cousin's interest. Nóra saved the situation by
grabbing a little girl in her arms and singing 'My Singing Bird'.

People exited after that, in a memory of mousses, soufflés,
and violent-looking, topsy-turvy chocolate cakes.

4

My cousin and I had a fight on Trophy Street, very near Nóra's
bed and breakfast house, and started hitting one another with
rosary beads. I broke my cousin's rosary beads and he bribed
me, by not telling his family about the sacrilege I'd committed,
to let him play Our Lady of Fatima in Nóra's place. A white bath
towel with a rose stripe on either end over him, he fell through
the long, low window when he made an appearance on it,
breaking it. The area around the big, broad street window
looked festered for a while after that, wood broken. My cousin
told his parents anyway about my having broken his beads and I
had to piously purchase him a new one, handing it to him
before he went into confession one day, when the boys of the

boys' national school were brought out like an army for their weekly confession, standing in regiments according to class outside the spindly spired church before being let into it. Nearby us, chalk statues, the Virgin Mary appeared to Bernadette of Lourdes.

5

Nóra began to die in earnest March 1961. She began to look gaunt, aged, a narrow ladder of a human being. Worry, ravagement were slapped on her forehead. She wore crimson lipstick to counter this effect. But it made her look more concerned, it made the waste of her face more draconian. But still she walked the town, quietly erect. Miles the circus man came more often to see her. Hair ran on the right side of his head like furze in bloom. He sat with her in the sitting room separated from the dining room by a wood partition which was sometimes open and sometimes closed. He sat beside comforting peat fires with her. I sat there too. We listened to her raw memories.

6

Nóra's father had died when she was very young and left her, an only child, with her mother, the bed and breakfast keeper, whom he'd taken out of Bin Lane, a pauper's daughter. There'd been a furore when he'd married her and people had warned him about her: 'She'll be the death of you.' And there were many women who claimed that she'd poisoned him. When Nóra was seventeen her mother had run away with an acrobat from the circus. The last Nóra saw of her mother whose auburn hair was tucked in a bun at the back. Nóra had closed up shop – the bed and breakfast house – and gone to England to work. It was during the war. She was a maid for a Jewish family in the East End, a rich Jewish family. A young man staying there, a relative, who crouched in a small room and wouldn't come out. He'd been a recent arrival. Nóra brought him lunch on silver trays. He'd been her first lover. Shortly after Yom Kippur, the Day of Atonement, 1945.

Daniel had very black curls which gathered around the pale, fearful effulgence of his features. He'd been very rich in Europe. He was very poor now, depending on relatives here. But there was an extravagant, a luxurious sensuality in his body, a redolence of ghostly but almost tangible perfumes. He'd been an actor in his country. He'd taken part in films. Something had vetted him, fate. Something had let him go. But in his eyes there was one particular film set: a street of skeletal buildings, only their fronts feigning reality, a sick calf of a moon over the street. It was the last film set he'd played on. He escaped down that street, making a getaway through the sick moon. There'd been many places in Europe which had harboured him. He'd been there for years. And then suddenly he'd arrived in England. 'I don't look Jewish,' he told Nóra, 'as an actor you can look anything.'

Actors stayed in Nóra's bed and breakfast house when she returned to Ireland and reopened it, actors from the travelling shows. They sang and danced for her and courted her. One man in a red kilt had danced a jig for her and then displayed his buttocks to a festive crowd after a successful performance of 'Dracula'. Nóra's mind in the early 1950s was on London, lustre on trays and picture frames there, Cheyne Walk camouflaged by film-set fog.

A young man had walked out with her there and when she'd had a few months of happiness she'd decided to leave, that, in an Irish way, enough was enough. She was afraid of having this token of happiness in her life spoiled. Anyway she thought the young man after all his suffering deserved better than her.

7

My mother was in and out of hospital at a great rate those years but in Nóra's trouble my mother befriended her and in her times out of hospital went to the bed and breakfast house frequently and commiserated with Nóra. Imminent death threw up an alliance between Nóra and my mother. My mother fortified Nóra with complaints about my father. The conversation between me and Nóra could not be daring with my mother there: whole worlds vanished when my mother was present and Nóra seemed just another anaemic, down-trodden item of this town. I was silenced by my mother every time I opened my mouth or dispensed with from the conversation by being absently told to go home.

Nóra took a long time to die so her death became a saga in the town; it spelt out the meaning of death and made people think of their own mortality. In her long and troubling death Nóra made people change their attitudes. My mother's attitudes changed most of all in that time. Miles, Nóra's lover, was accepted for what he was, and even with prurient wonder that a dying woman was having these carnal visits. There was no longer consternation when a newly put up crimson curtain in place of the wooden partition swished and Miles entered the scene in the sitting room. My mother's head was thrown back only, her neck muscles emphasized. Nóra gradually lost that cardboard quality in my mother's presence and began to breathe as a real human being. At the same time my mother became real. Two women, I'd often leave them, and slink home to bed. That was the last time, those last months of Nóra's life, that I saw my mother open to and even energized by possibilities beyond this town. As I crept out of the front door sometimes I'd hear my mother laugh – like a young girl.

I was totally confused by this new identity for my mother. I had long buried any hopes for her. So I accepted her in this new state of effervescence as another friend to the dying Nóra, and I in no way attempted to develop possibilities from this change, this awkward radicalization. I ignored the one chance I ever had to get to know my mother in order to keep apace with Nóra's moods, not realizing that I'd changed too. I was a young man, aged thirteen, in long trousers, in spring 1964, keeping abreast with Nóra as we sauntered through the fair green.

8

When Nóra ended up in the bed on the first floor Miles vanished; he stopped coming. It was the summer and then it was mainly me and my mother. I'd stop for endless hours and talk with her. From outside we'd hear children's voices. There was a bed of wallflowers in the narrow yard. Sometimes in the heat they threw colours on to the white wall. Nóra talked. She talked a lot. She espoused the colours of the sharper fragments of her life. I wore a pale pink T-shirt. Occasionally her spindly white fingers would go absently to my chest.

Turning to me, more consciously, she once told me, 'There are lovely colours in your eyes.' Maritime shadows on the walls, a few triangular white shapes – like yachts.

Towards late summer a whingeing file of women in scarves came, townswomen who always came to a house when death was near. They never had the imagination to get to know a person before they were about to die; they specialized in rancorous gossip and in death. Their heads bent, in scarves, they were Russian women. They created an incoherent babble that might have been Russian. I was ousted for long hours. But I always managed to wend my way back to the source, to Nóra alone. Hair was striped on either side of her head now, lank witch's hair. She still sat erect in the bed my mother made for her, by the pillows my mother ceaselessly purified for her. She looked out, staring straight at the river of her life.

9

Between the houses of our street and the river were outhouses. That summer a little Indian chief suddenly appeared on top of the shell of one of these houses, a wild crest of ruby feathers on him. It was a little boy dressed up. Protestants played cricket in a field by the river and further on were the mental hospital buildings. The train ran on the other side of the river. That train, now that I was aged thirteen, ran into dreams of marigold pubic hair, into the sudden realization of a soaking manifestation on the bed.

10

Miles turned up in November, just before Nóra died. There was a great drama of reconciliation. He walked in the door when my mother was in the house. He'd grown a beard, a very toxic and scarce-looking beard. If anything he was fatter and he trundled with more difficulty. Nóra, in the bed, clung to his huge waist. My mother had purchased a picture of St Thérèse of Lisieux, all in shades of dolorous brown, on a recent train excursion to Dublin and put it up in the room earlier that night, St Thérèse carrying a bouquet of creamy brown, almost white, roses. Such was the passion with which Nóra clung to Miles's waist that the picture, not properly put up, came down, one electric bouquet of tiny glass particles under the bed, the picture standing drunkenly on the floor, which a few days before had sat with dignity on a shop wall on Aston Quay, Dublin, looking out at the monk-browns of the houses and the contaminated greys of the winter sky. St Thérèse was not meant to be brought west because when she was put up again she fell down again but this time when Nóra's body was laid out and this time, without glass, her paper breast ripped and the bouquet ripped and the paper curved within the frame – erotically even.

11

Miles went crazy. Or he pretended to go crazy, hollering. 'I'm a traitor. I'm a traitor,' were the words that reached the town from the staircase. Later that night he went to a pub and banged his head on the urinal wall and slumped unconscious on the floor. Being from a circus he wore a black tie with saffron in it at Nóra's funeral.

12

Miles acted out our grief for us so we were silenced. I stood for a long time by Nóra's coffin in the alcove of the church through which November winds blew. Spindly candles burned beside the coffin.

Coffins were always brought here before being moved up in the church for the mass for the dead. There were preliminary prayers here. I'd been waiting here long before the prayers and the audience. Miles came and blubbered. His beard had disappeared overnight and his face, newly shaven, was a pale cartoon. He walked behind the coffin to the graveyard. In his tie with saffron in it he looked heraldic, like someone honouring the birthday of a city or a mummer on Stephen's Day who cried obsequies for the wren.

13

Nóra left the bed and breakfast house to my mother and under my mother's management it became a holiday place mainly for priests. Old priests came in summer and rummaged about and snarled to themselves. My mother hired a man rather than a woman to help her and he served the priests breakfast in a suit and also brought mid-morning coffee and biscuits to them in his suit. The house was a kind of elephants' graveyard for priests. Towards the late 1960s there was a kind of dormancy about it. That man seemed to be always standing on stairways with a tray of biscuits, a claret tie on him and an insipid smile sponged on to his moustached face. Movement in the house became more and more silent. People tip-toed. People whispered. Eventually everyone seemed to have lost their voice so religious was the atmosphere. St Thérèse, favourite of the priests, stood by a lower stairway. The man my mother had hired had begun to smell, a sickly, moth-ball innuendo from him, the decay of treacly celibacy. The summer he had a heart attack and died he wore a grin as if he was being continually photographed. He looked half-witted. He died carrying a tray with a plate of marshmallows on it down the stairs, past St Thérèse. Russia invaded Czechoslovakia the following day. I went to the city the following year.

14

The long, languorous, imprisoned summer before I went to the city the daftest of all events occurred, an event well within the continuum of Nóra's story. Nóra's mother turned up in the dining room of the bed and breakfast house. She'd been living in the South of France with a retired Jewish acrobat for years. He had just recently died. She decided to dig up the world of early life. Her hair was still auburn, still in a lax bun at the back, the folds of her skin were a Mediterranean clay from the sun; she was decked out, under her thin coat, in a dress that had a furious leafy pattern on it. She'd lived among her husband's people for years. The English of Bin Lane was penetrated by a French accent. But altogether, despite age, there was an enviable radiance about her; she was a sun-spot in the dining room. She held up well against the news of her daughter's death. She stood there, negotiating with the past. An old priest walked by her with a fishing rod and a sealed jar of squirming worms.

15

The visit of this witch, this Cassandra, was the last straw for my mother. She swooned under it. She couldn't bear being in the house after that. By meeting Nóra's mother she felt she'd touched the roots of poverty in this town. My mother owned the house of the daughter of a former resident of Bin Lane. This house now led into a labyrinthine story; Bin Lane, the circus, the Mediterranean, a few Jewish houses in a street by the Mediterranean. It was all too much. The house was purchased by someone who turned it into a petrol station. Nóra's mother returned to the South of France, after a long stay with Jewish friends of her husband in a cottage on Rathgar Avenue in Dublin. I visited her there sometimes on Sunday afternoons. She spoke French to me. She'd translated all the gibberish of her childhood in Bin Lane, of expeditions for eels in the shallows of the river, into French. I wasn't staying far away. My mother had me incarcerated in another cottage with three priests who were supposed to make sure for the three years I was at university that I didn't misbehave. After three years with the priests I escaped. White cherry blossom was in bloom outside the cottage the day I escaped.

I had my fling after that; late, I lived it up. I began to hate my mother and punish her in every way possible. My girlfriend had a baby but then, being from an upper-class Dublin family, left me, taking the baby, going back to her upper-class family, denying our life together, the room in Brighton Square with two Olympian lovers on the wall, lovers flying over a robust Pre-Raphaelite cherry tree in blossom.

I joined the theatre world. I lived in a tiny, famished room beside a large theatre. Someone scrawled in crimson lipstick on the mirror there one night: 'Gregory is best in drag.'

I noticed, not one, but three statues of Our Lady of Fatima on a window-sill in Whitefriar Street the day I left Ireland.

16

The London stage greeted me but then I got tired of the stage and turned to other outlets, the cinema, the television screen. There was some basic compulsion lacking in me to go on acting and I went to live in seclusion in a cottage on the east coast of England, by the sea. Intrusions from Ireland traumatized me. Visits from brothers, people who thought they were overseers in my life. I became a friend of the local vicar and worked with young people, giving drama workshops. That was my happiest time, away from ambition, the score with Ireland even. But then my landlord died and my cottage was taken from me and I returned to London and I resorted to odd jobs in theatre, getting good parts by accident, a modicum of fame. I was the face on the poster that sometimes unsettled visitors from our town to London. I reached an equilibrium with life, not trying too desperately, sometimes having money, sometimes having none.

When a circus pitched in the park opposite my room one day I knew I had to move and so I started travelling, taking a bus from Victoria bus station to the South of France.

17

An old woman and the heat; her ancestors might have lived here for hundreds of years. She was from my town. We had a lot in common and a lot separating us. Her knobbly, ever more activated, arm linked mine. We walked a lot in the streets. I knew that summer where runaways from our town ended up.

There were fireworks over the sea one night. One particular crimson plume grew bigger and bigger, swimming out in all directions. Anybody who'd gone away with the circus from our town ended up here, troubled, a few phoney gipsies trying to read your palm for money and a Jewish boy who looked like a gypsy standing against the wheel of fortune in the funfair. He was the grandson of Nóra's mother. She'd created a new lineage. Joseph led me through the more dizzy parts of town. In a way I constantly wondered at, I was with a relative of Nóra and I was behaving as an adolescent with him, the adolescent I'd never been allowed to be. Whatever else there was that summer, I said goodbye at the end of it to the woman from Bin Lane whose dun skin seemed to remember only the sun and the confluences of the sun but whose pale blue eyes had seemed until recently attacked by and troubled by the memory of a daughter she'd left behind. I was her forgiveness. That's why I'd come. And she was my wisdom. She taught me that grey Irish rivers could become, however high the price, however unstable the mood, the intoxicated shade of the Mediterranean that day.

18

For years when I went back to Ireland I went to the florid sea. I ignored the town with the river. When my father died I had to go back there I suppose. He died when I was earning a lot of money. I was wearing a fashionable jacket. I thought of the crimson worm potion he always carried, like a strange, festive champagne.

My mother died, by contrast, in the year of Chernobyl, when I was in Prague, having run away there with the first sizeable portion of money I'd earned for a long time. I didn't make her funeral and only returned to the town after her funeral.

My fat cousin was the only one who would speak to me. He was a friar now, running a home for delinquent boys in a nearby town, a small, modern house taken over by a charitable organization.

Shunned by almost all I walked by the river behind the town and I could see the mosaic of the houses of our town. I lived now in south-east London, often on the violent edge of poverty; an

Irish tinker encampment nearby. I realized, walking by the river, that I'd lost my confidence in the last few years; brothers who worked in England came to me and almost tried to dictate to me the kind of personality I should have. They had penetrated into my self-confidence. I had given up some of the flow I'd had after first arriving in England. It was time to find the river in me again, regardless.

The tinker encampment near me was one sanctioned by the local borough; they'd even built a few small houses. I sometimes went there and chatted to the inhabitants. They knew my town. It was the serpentine river they always identified it by.

People had begun building the town by a curl in the river: a ford. I was near that ford now. And I looked back and saw Nóra's back window.

I'd been offered a part in a film recently: a big project. I was wondering whether to take it. Coming back made the decision easy. I remembered Nóra in the spring of the year she died, when Miles had let her down for the first time, not turning up for a dinner dance he was supposed to accompany her to, walking down Trophy Street, dressed in saffron, going to the annual civic guards' dinner dance by herself, green eye-shadow on her and a cinematic style about her gait – she walked as if she were an image from a cataclysmic but ruinous film, all dressed up to beguile the audience on the first night and assuage the memory when all the bad notices had collected and been burnt individually to nervous, brown, malformed items of ash.

I went back to the house where I'd grown up, determined that I'd make my own film one day, a film that would have that woman in it and express her life and the look on her face on Trophy Street when I, a young adolescent, had called after her and she turned and I cried, only half-heard, 'Nóra, Nóra, don't die.'

19

I went to bed and suddenly became abashed by my flight of fancy, by my poetic ambition. But Nóra, the film heroine, was instilled in me and I dreamt of her that night. She turned up, over a sand dune in the South of France, her saffron dress on and a parasol over her head, her hair auburn and scratches of poppies on either side of her. She was calling to me. I was trying to hear in the light on the beach which was that of a nuclear blast.

'Gregory, Gregory, don't die,' I woke up mumbling to myself. The river outside was rose at dawn, it held a palpitation of rose in the mirror of its surface. The river carried this colour into the distance, towards the mental hospital buildings. Those buildings couldn't muster much of an air of harmony. They ran, decrepit things, into the fields. They seemed to nuzzle at the green of the fields. Tomorrow I would be far from the green of those fields and from this family house which promised fecundity once as all family houses do at some stage. But I forgave it this promise and it forgave me, I think, there among the pale yellow wallpaper, my shortcomings.

My former girlfriend came down from Dublin to see me that day, in her navy Peugeot, bringing my son. They'd stopped at a barn-like bar for an hour where you could either take a road to Sligo or jut off on the narrow, surprisingly primitive Galway road. They'd boosted themselves with country and western music in the bar before resuming the journey. My son had thick chestnut hair; he wore a jersey of crocheted diamonds. He was not interested in me, shrugged off any interest in me almost immediately and turned his attention to a dead, banshee-like tree outside which frantically hopping jackdaws had made their home. When Nóra was alive that tree would have been in bloom this time of year. It was a visual our house shared with Nóra's house. It had connected our back views. The son went off to the town; in Reg's he had steak and chips and on coming back he described how the ketchup had sprayed over the bountiful, fleshy chips – like blood from a bull just shot. The boy becoming more demonstrative in his lack of interest in me his mother took him back to Dublin. She was an art teacher now. She'd never married. The last I saw of her was the back of her buttercup hair as she bent to get into the car, in a white blouse and long, tweed, fussily patterned skirt. I thought afterwards that she looked like a soprano who might have sung a song for us.

I turned my attention to the tree at the back of the house. I saw it not as it was now but as it had been then, in unfettered, friendly bloom.

20

A friend drove to the South of France that Christmas: I went with him. I had to make a road other than the Dublin–Galway road my own and I thought this one would be ideal, the road from Lyons to Marseilles. The weather was warm. I wasn't sure of the cast of characters who would be waiting for me: Nóra's mother, Joseph. Whatever the risks I had to put a stake on a few human beings again. Ironic that it should be on people who were, however you looked at it, a tributary of childhood. Yes, and I had been perusing the books of French grammar I'd kept in damp places of London rooms for years.

The sun was a dash of white on the Mediterranean on Christmas Day. I walked towards it. The freckles on the face of Nóra's mother were coarse as she watched me, all chopped up as if she'd got them from standing by the river for a summer long ago. Her eyes were vague. What was she looking at? The Mediterranean or the shallows of a river in summer heat as an epic multitude of the poor attacked the river in search of eels.

21

That dream continues to haunt me, Nóra rising from the land side of a sand dune, in her saffron dress, a parasol over her head. She looks to the sea, halting. Although I always see her by the sea, on top of a sand dune, the auburn of her hair and the prescience of her freckles are from the river. She is someone who's made the voyage from a green river-world to this baffling, pale landscape. She acknowledges her debt to the river by the look of pain in her eyes as she confronts the sea. Although happy, although fulfilled, she will never quite be at home here. There will always be a gap and maybe that gap will be creative at times, the sensuality overwhelming. But that sensuality will always flounder with a memory of some continuous betrayal being undertaken, some loyalty being undone. She is, on these cold, grey days, my link with the river.

22

The weather was warm by the Mediterranean last Christmas. I swam a lot in the sea. Sometimes I coaxed Joseph in. The old lady had us bring a table to the edge of the sea one day and we ate there – the sun was hurling sticks on Joseph's cheekbones. He looked at me. It was not the look of a stranger. We were, the sea lapping at the legs of the table and at the legs of the chairs, the sun going down early on us and burnishing those waves which were threatening to carry us away, we were, by decree of a river followed long ago and celebrated now with wine, we were, the last of the sun bashing at a bottle of wine on top of a drowning table, we were, astride the threads of blue and white T-shirts, under the spectre of a tree in full bloom, a family-tableau after all.